Metaphorosis

March 2021

Beautifully made speculative fiction

Also from Metaphorosis

<u>Verdage</u>

Reading 5X5 x2: Duets
Score – an SFF symphony
Reading 5X5: Readers' Edition
Reading 5X5: Writers' Edition

<u>Metaphorosis Magazine</u>

Metaphorosis: Best of 20xx
Metaphorosis 20xx: The Complete Stories
annual issues, from 2016

Monthly issues

<u>Plant Based Press</u>

Best Vegan Science Fiction & Fantasy
annual issues, from 2016

from B. Morris Allen:
Susurrus
Allenthology: Volume I
Tocsin: and other stories
Start with Stones: collected stories
Metaphorosis: a collection of stories

Metaphorosis

March 2021

---

edited by
B. Morris Allen

ISSN: 2573-136X (online)
ISBN: 978-1-64076-195-7 (e-book)
ISBN: 978-1-64076-196-4 (paperback)

Metaphorosis
a magazine of speculative fiction
from
Metaphorosis Publishing

Neskowin

March 2021

Spells for Going Forth by Day

V.G. Campen

I find Anubis about a mile past the Amtrak rails, where the sawgrass of the New Jersey salt marsh turns to swaying reeds of papyrus. He stands on a muddy creek bank holding a fishing pole and, though eight years have passed since I last saw him, he looks the same—a slender youth with the head of a jet-black jackal.

Anubis catches sight of me and morphs into fully human form, the most difficult shape for him to maintain. He turns away and begins pulling in his fishing line.

"Anubis," I call out. "It's me, Grace." At that he looks up and gives a short bark of surprise.

"Grace, a thousand pardons," he says, striding toward me, jackal-headed once again. "I did not recognize my little princess, all grown up." We embrace, and I inhale the scents of sandalwood and sun-warmed fur.

"Where is Matthew?" he asks, gazing over my shoulder, searching for my brother.

My throat tightens. "Hospital," I whisper. "Car accident."

Anubis holds me at arm's length and stares into my eyes, then nuzzles my face with his slender muzzle, casting about for the scent of death.

"He's not dead," I say.

"No," Anubis agrees. "Not dead." He releases me. "Come, I need help with these fish." He kneels and pulls a string of perch and mullet from the creek, then we push through the reeds to a clearing atop a slight rise where Anubis has created a camp out of detritus dredged from the tidal creeks. Plastic chairs sit near a rusty metal drum that serves as a fire pit. I set to work gutting the fish, splitting their cool slick bodies from anus to operculum and drawing forth the entrails.

As children, Matthew and I spent long summer days with Anubis in the marsh, away from the chaos of our daily lives. He taught us how to set a bird's broken wing and mend a terrapin's cracked shell, gave anatomy lessons using the bodies of egrets and voles. Little wonder I'm now in med school and Matthew is—was—a science teacher. But one thing Anubis never taught us, despite our pleas, was mummification. "It is not a trick," he'd said. "It is a sacred ritual, an honor for the living and the dead."

Anubis stirs the ashes in the fire pit, uncovering smoldering wood and coaxing forth small flames. I sit listening to crickets and songbirds as he grills the fish. Feral cats gather around us, half-hidden in the vegetation, their eyes flashing green-gold in the shadows. Anubis breaks our silence. "It is good to see you, little one. That day you chased Matthew into the marsh is a treasure in my memory."

As usual, Matthew had forged a path and I'd followed. Three years older than I, restless and curious, he'd snuck out of our tiny apartment one Saturday morning while our mother slept, exhausted after another 60-hour workweek laboring at two menial jobs. I'd watched through the kitchen window as Matthew trotted across the parking lot, ignoring the group of men who gathered to smoke and drink no matter the hour. He'd clambered down the sloping concrete side of the storm water ditch that marked the boundary between asphalt and tidal marsh and disappeared from view. I hesitated, trying not to care, then grabbed a sweatshirt and ran after him.

I caught sight of my brother at the end of the ditch, where a trickle of dirty water spilled into the marsh. Matthew, hearing my sneakers slapping along the concrete behind him, sprinted into the grass and I followed, not knowing to stay on high ground. I floundered along the twisting creek beds and soon became mired knee-deep in mud exposed by the receding tide. Disoriented and panicked, I screamed for Matthew. When he found me, I was on the creek bank with my arms wrapped around a lean black dog who smelled of sandalwood and dust.

Anubis lifts the fish off the grill and begins singing in a low voice, summoning a dozen cats in from the sedge for their dinner. Grey, tabby, ginger, black—each one is sleek and elegant, wearing a collar made of bone and glass beads. While they eat, Anubis and I trade stories about Matthew. Even as an adult he found the time to visit the marsh, while I stayed away, succumbing to the demands of med school and the seduction of living in Manhattan.

"And what of Matthew now?" Anubis asks.

"He's on life support." *Irreversible coma*, to use a medical term. A *gomer*, in the slang of residents and interns. I start crying.

Anubis leans forward and licks at the tears on my cheek, though his amber eyes remain dry. Jackals do not weep. "Matthew was not afraid of anything in this life," he says. "You need not fear for him now. When his heart is weighed in the afterlife, it will be lighter than Maat's feather, filled with good deeds."

"But they want *me* to make the decision, to stop the ventilator. To let him go." I swipe my nose on my sleeve like a child. "And I still need him."

"It is no kindness to keep him in a world he cannot fully inhabit," Anubis says, "alone and apart from all he knows." A smoke-gray cat with green eyes leaps into his lap. Anubis strokes her head and adjusts her collar.

"Anubis, I'm a fraud," I blurt out. "How can I become a physician, how can I presume, if I can't handle this?"

Anubis stares across the marsh at a bank of thunderclouds massing on the horizon. "Perhaps, on this day, you should think of Matthew first."

My sorrow turns to anger, quick as the silvered turn of a minnow. "Do I disappoint you?" I stand abruptly, causing cats to scatter and dart back into the reeds. "Forget it. Forget me. I don't know why I thought the noble Lord of the Necropolis would have sympathy for one mortal's struggle. All *you* care about are dusty old museum pieces."

"Those are the remains of people who worshipped me. You would do well to show respect."

"*Dust*," I shout. "Why are you even here? Hiding in a makeshift camp, keeping company with feral cats and stray children?"

Anubis goes still. His fur darkens beyond black, draining the light around him and creating an inky nimbus. My rage dissipates and I fear I've gone too far. As children we never questioned Anubis's presence in the marsh, accepting his stories of following sacred treasures plundered from Egyptian tombs and dispersed to collections across the world—including, of course, New York's Metropolitan Museum of Antiquities.

"You are correct," he says. "What remains is dust. I escorted their spirits to Osiris and set them on the path to the afterlife. My work in this world is done." Anubis exhales slowly, still gazing at the horizon. "My child, do you know what happens to gods when they are no longer revered?"

I shake my head and stay silent.

"Old gods are replaced by new gods," Anubis says. "Roman, Greek, Byzantine, each in turn with different ways of life and death. And now I am trapped."

I hear a subtle shift in his tone, a longing that pierces his customary reserve. "Trapped? Why are you trapped?"

"Because I have forgotten. I no longer remember how to pass between worlds and step upon the pathway. I do not have a tomb illustrated with maps, filled with inscriptions and incantations for my soul. No one builds a tomb for a god."

Three days later I return to the marsh carrying a daypack and a canvas shopping bag. Anubis sits cross-legged on the ground, plaiting a basket from slender blades of sea grass. When I up-end my bag and dump out tins of supermarket cat food, he raises an eyebrow and, though the sun is still high overhead, begins singing home the cats.

"I apologize for my words and behavior at our last meeting," I say. "I showed disrespect when you were trying to guide me." Anubis nods and returns to his basket-making while I dole out whitefish and tuna to the milling cats. When each has been served, I settle on the ground and pull from the backpack a heavy book, its cover embossed with the insignia of the Museum of Antiquities.

"What is this?" Anubis asks. His ears prick with curiosity. Matthew and I had often brought books to the marsh, both textbooks and novels, but I'd never thought to ask what Anubis wished to see.

"We call it the *Egyptian Book of the Dead.*" I hand it to him and he rubs a finger over the raised lettering.

"A strange gift." He flips quickly through the introductory pages, baring his teeth at the photographs of mummies and sarcophagi, slowing when he reaches glossy reproductions of fragmented papyri and peeling murals. "It is the *Spells for Going Forth by Day,*" he says, "and fragments of the *Book of Caverns* and the *Book of Dark Waters.*"

"Can it set you on the path to your afterlife?"

He places the book in his lap and resumes plaiting the seagrass. "I think not. These are fragments from versions written centuries apart. Fragments out of context cannot, unfortunately, compensate for centuries of forgetting."

"There's more. Look at this." I extend a brochure advertising the Museum's newest exhibit: a full-sized recreation of a Fifth Dynasty royal burial chamber, one that had remained sealed and untouched until the last decade. "It's not the real thing, but with laser scanning and digitizing and I don't even understand it all, they recreated every surface down to the smallest detail—all the murals, every prayer and incantation."

Anubis reviews the brochure, then places it carefully inside the book and returns to weaving, his face impassive. The cats finish eating and begin cleaning their whiskers as the first evening star appears. Soon it will be too dark to hike safely out of the marsh, yet I remain sitting until Anubis puts the finished basket aside and I can no longer hold my tongue. "If I get you to the museum, to this tomb, is it enough?"

"I believe it might be," he says. "However, your duty is to Matthew, not to me."

"Let me help you. Please. Then I will be ready to help Matthew, I promise."

It is well past nightfall when Anubis finally responds. He hands me the basket, so tightly and perfectly woven it will hold water. "A gift for my princess," he says, and in the giving and accepting of this gift our agreement is made.

I spend the night in a chair by the fire pit, slapping at mosquitoes and dozing fitfully. Anubis, in the form of a jackal, curls on a bed of rushes with the *Book of the Dead* by his side. At first daylight I kneel and massage the muscles in his neck and shoulders, a familiarity he tolerates only when in jackal form. He yawns and blinks. "Every dawn is a victory," he says. "Remember that, Grace. Every day of life a triumph over the chaos of night."

Anubis huddles in the back seat of my rented car, his jackal head hidden under a blanket. He has spent the past weeks poring over the *Book of the Dead* and has become solemn and aloof. He no longer speaks, communicating instead by nods and glances. I maneuver through Manhattan traffic and pay an absurd amount to park in a garage adjacent to the museum. When Anubis shrugs off the blanket, he is fully human, though his face remains oddly canine, with deep amber eyes and pointed ears. Appearing in public is risky; in moments of emotion or stress his jackal head can unexpectedly re-assert itself. He wears a sweatshirt, lose khaki pants, and tennis shoes. No belt. Nothing metal that might set off a detector and incur a pat-down. I doubt he could maintain his form if touched disrespectfully. I hand him sunglasses and a hipster fedora to complete the costume.

We arrive in the museum's ornate 19th century entry hall a mere ten minutes before the final visitors are admitted, an hour before the museum closes. A guard rises from her chair behind the security table and points to my backpack. Instead of handing it over, I upend the bag and spill out a confusion of books, cosmetics, and keys, chattering inanely all the while. At the same time Anubis holds up his hands, palms outward, to show he carries nothing. The guard nods and Anubis saunters through the metal detector while I recover my belongings. Our plan is simple, based on clichéd movie tropes: wait until closing time and hope we are the last visitors in the Hall of Ancient Egypt, so that Anubis can enter the replicated tomb alone. If needed, I will create a diversion to distract any lingering visitors or nearby museum staff.

I rejoin Anubis on the far side of the rotunda, behind the massive skeletons of a *T. rex* and a triceratops locked in eternal battle, and we head toward an exhibit on fossils from the Gobi Desert. We'll wait to enter the Egyptian display, to avoid upsetting Anubis and drawing unwanted attention. In front of us, a toddler carried by his mother stares at Anubis over her shoulder. "Doggy," he says, and Anubis smiles a pointy-toothed grin and morphs for an instant to jackal-head, causing the child to shriek with laughter and allowing me, for a single breath, to see once again the old Anubis, my patient teacher and friend.

But the momentary shift in his head sends the fedora and sunglasses tumbling to the floor. I crouch to fetch them and, when I rise, Anubis is disappearing into the Hall of Ancient Egypt through a wide doorway flanked by granite obelisks. I mutter a curse and follow. Thankfully, the exhibit is nearly empty. One couple remains, busy posing next to burial masks and golden amulets, intent on documenting their visit with selfies. Beyond them, the recreated tomb occupies an elevated platform, dramatically lit by hidden spotlights. Velvet ropes delineate a pathway to the tomb's entrance steps.

Anubis has stopped in the middle of the room, in front of a large glass enclosure containing a Middle Kingdom mummy case, the lid removed to reveal the time-ravaged body. Canopic jars holding the dead man's lungs, liver, stomach, and intestines rest on wooden pedestals nearby. Anubis presses one hand against the glass, his head flickering rapidly between man and jackal. The light in the room dims. Shadows creep from under display cases and stretch over the marble floor toward the tomb.

The couple, startled, turn to see the Lord of the Necropolis striding toward them—jackal-headed, clad in loincloth and golden headpiece, trailing folds of darkness like a ceremonial robe. They run for the exit and Anubis follows, toppling the granite obelisks behind them to block the doorway. Alarms blare.

Anubis moves toward the tomb, barely visible now in the deepening shadows. I think he pauses and looks back at me before stepping across the threshold, but I cannot be certain. The darkness withdraws like a receding tide and the light returns, hazy with dust created by security guards clambering over granite rubble. They find me sobbing on the floor and, assuming my grief is fear, kneel to comfort me.

The tabloid headlines are campy and awful: *Nightmare at the Museum* and Mummy's Revenge! The stories describe the toppled obelisks and provide unofficial photos of the wreckage, as well as a single blurry photo of the masked figure who chased visitors from the exhibit. The museum, no surprise, declines comment and refuses to release any security camera footage.

I read each article to Matthew as I sit by his hospital bed holding his limp hand. When the stories are done, when there is nothing more to tell Matthew about Anubis, I summon the attending physician and watch as she disconnects his respirator. There are no canopic jars waiting for his organs; they will be dispatched with equal reverence to patients in need of transplants.

I leave the hospital and drive to the marsh, where I walk for miles beyond the Amtrak rails. The reeds remain reeds. There is no papyrus. The feral cats I glimpse are skinny and skittish, and none wears a collar of glass beads. Anubis is gone from this world. What is lost can never be replaced, yet the sun still warms my face and the creeks still pulse with the tides. I am at peace in this narrow space between earth and sky, once again willing to endure the chaos of the night for the promise of another dawn.

See V.G. Campen's story "Spells for Going Forth by Day" online at Metaphorosis.
If you liked it, leave a comment. Authors love that!
Remember to subscribe to our e-mail updates so you'll know when new stories are posted.

About the story

Some years ago, from the window of a passenger train traveling the eastern U.S., I watched a jackal trot across a shallow creekbed and disappear into waist-high marsh grass. In reality it was likely a stray dog, or possibly a coyote, as jackals are not native to North America. But the idea of a jackal living alone in the tidal flats felt both beautiful and lonely.

I drafted "Spells for Going Forth by Day" when I was coming to terms with the death of a loved one, when I was grappling with the pain and guilt that we humans inflict upon ourselves. The story to me is fundamentally hopeful, and less about death than about having the courage to live in a challenging and impermanent world.

Regarding the actual writing, the first draft was much too complicated for a piece of this length, with backstory and flashbacks shoehorned into the narrative. That baggage detracted from the pacing and impact of the story. It's an issue I struggle with: learning to edit and streamline short stories for best effect. The scene in the museum draw upon my childhood fantasy of staying overnight in a natural history museum (a fantasy I haven't entirely abandoned).

A question for the author

Q: How does writing speculative fiction affect your daily life (not as a writer but as a person)?

A: Writing speculative fiction—and reading the works of others—is like calisthenics for the imagination. It opens the mind to the fantastic. What if the weather were sentient? What if whales abandoned the ocean for the skies? On a deeper level, writing speculative fiction has increased my curiosity about, and empathy for, other members of the contrary species known as *Homo sapiens*.

About the author

V.G. Campen is an introvert who has learned to act like an extrovert. She lives in North Carolina with one spouse, numerous animals, and an alter-ego who writes horror.

Going Home

Martin Westlake

The eerie howl of the Ekranoplan's jet engines echoed around the city's early morning streets. Dimitriy's stomach lurched involuntarily. A ground effect craft, they called it, designed to be a troop carrier, now recycled as a passenger craft, plying the route between Derbent and Astrakhan. The relic, all stubby wings and a massive, V-shaped tail, howled there and back three times a day. He loathed it, but it was the only way he could get to the laboratory in Astra.

Every Monday morning for over a year, Dimitriy had suffered the same torment of emotions. Anastasia said nothing anymore as they kissed. "Think of the children," she had said in the old days, before she'd realised entreaties were useless. "They need their father." He missed the whole school week. Sasha, the younger, still greeted him with affection on Saturday mornings, but Andrei, now in his teens, had become increasingly sullen. Dimitriy wanted to tell him how sorry he felt, but the truth was that he didn't. Guilty, yes; sad, yes, in a bittersweet sort of way; but not sorry.

Then there was the Ekranoplan. Anastasia had been unable to leave Derbent when Dimitriy had taken on the Astrakhan job and he had accepted that. The car trip took ten hours in the summer and in the winter the roads were frequently impassable. No, the only viable means of getting there was the Ekranoplan. He would never get used to it, though. Whenever there was the slightest hint of a breeze, his heart dropped, for the monstrous thing could only take off facing into the wind, and that meant riding the incoming waves, like a ship. Once it was up in the air the ride was smooth, but how he hated the take off! The only thing that made the mixture of sadness, guilt and fear worthwhile every Monday morning was a euphoric sense of anticipation; the knowledge that he would soon once again be where he most desired to be.

His path through the sleepy streets to the Ekranoport took him past his old workplace, the Caspian Gates Secondary School, reminding him of the day it had all begun. He'd stayed behind to help a group of fifteen-year-olds, then hurried home. A tall, thin, grey-suited, sallow-faced man was waiting for him outside the main entrance to their block of flats. A cigarette bobbed on his lower lip as he spoke. He seemed oblivious to the February cold, though both men's breath clouded about them.

"Semenov?" he said.

Dimitriy nodded.

"Could we talk?" said the man, nodding towards a bar.

There was something about him — not furtive, but a sense of secrecy all the same. The man bought two vodkas and they sat at a scuffed table.

"To your health," he said, raising his glass. He stubbed out his cigarette in an old dented aluminium ashtray and lit another. "Ivanov," he said. "Rear Admiral Anatoly Ivanov, Caspian Flotilla, Astrakhan."

"There's been a mistake," said Dimitriy.

Ivanov shook his head. He gestured to a passing waiter and ordered two more vodkas.

"I shouldn't stay," said Dimitriy.

"Tell me, Dimitriy Semenov," Ivanov said; "how much do you earn?"

"Enough," said Dimitriy.

"Why are you a teacher?" Ivanov leaned forward over the table. "You are a brilliant physicist with a top doctoral thesis in Biology and Materials Sciences from Moscow State University and yet you hide yourself away at the Caspian Gates Secondary School teaching low-grade mathematics to misfits."

"My wife...," Dimitriy began.

"We know all about your wife," Ivanov said.

"It's time I left," Dimitriy said.

"Sit down," said the Admiral, gesturing with his half-empty vodka glass. "What I mean is that we know she has all her family here. That's why you're here, isn't it?"

Dimitriy said nothing.

Ivanov leaned over the table again. "The motherland calls, comrade."

Motherland! Comrade! Dimitriy knew immediately that the job had to be some sort of secret military work.

"It's not what you think, Semenov," the Admiral continued. "If I told you now, you wouldn't believe me."

Dimitriy inadvertently looked into his empty glass. Ivanov flagged the waiter down and ordered two more vodkas.

"No!" said Dimitriy.

"For the road."

The Admiral toyed with his cigarette lighter, an old-fashioned metal model with a flip top and a thick wick. Then he looked up at Dimitry. "Interested?" he asked. "We'll pay you four times what you are getting at that dump of a school."

"The catch?" said Dimitriy.

Ivanov drank off the remainder of his vodka and placed the glass down gently on the tabletop.

"You'd have to come to Astra, Monday to Friday. We'd cover your board and lodging."

"How would I…?"

As if to anticipate his question, the unmistakable howl of the evening return

Ekranoplan came to them through the thin glass window.

Ivanov reached into his pocket, drew out an envelope and placed it on the table.

"Your ticket's in there. This coming Monday. The seven-thirty departure. When you get to Astra, make your way to the Moskva Hotel. A room has been booked in your name. I'll join you there for lunch. It's half-term. The school won't miss you."

Back home, after the children had gone to bed, sitting in the low light at the melamine kitchen table, he and Anastasia had discussed the offer in earnest whispers. He had doubts, but she was logical and reassuring. The money was important. With the kids growing, it would be good if they could rent somewhere larger. If he didn't like the work, whatever it was, he could always return to his teaching. What did they have to lose?

Dimitriy had been travelling to Astra for just over two months when Anastasia first put the question to him. He had known it must come. She had nodded and accepted so mildly when he'd first explained that he couldn't talk about his work, but who could blame her, now that the yearning had started? She chose a Saturday evening. The children were in bed. The classical music radio channel was on, and she'd put a cloth and a candle on the dinner table. They talked about Sasha and Andrei, and then about her family. At the end of the meal, Anastasia took Dimitriy's hands across the table. *Here it comes*, he thought. But she simply looked into his eyes and asked if he felt all right. She'd told him he seemed preoccupied, as if his mind were elsewhere.

He'd laughed. "I'm fine," he'd said.

How could he tell her? Even if he had told her, she wouldn't have believed him.

The second time, Anastasia had been more direct. Dimitriy had just returned.

"Did you miss us?" she asked.

"Of course!"

"Really?"

She went back to the kitchen. There was no cloth and no candle on the table. Over the meal, her replies were monosyllabic. Afterwards, he went to help her with the washing up, but she insisted on doing it alone. He sat on the sofa and waited until she emerged, drying her hands on a tea towel.

"Dima," she said, "are you sure you're not having a relationship of some sort in Astra?"

Astrakhan was on a broad river, not a sea. Its waterways gave the impression the city was floating. Unlike Derbent, there were no hills behind, and no citadel looming over the city. Rather, the great Trinity Cathedral soared upwards, with its gold-capped green domes. Astrakhan was flat and expansive. Being there gave Dimitry a sense of a new beginning. He hadn't realised, until he first set foot in the place, how oppressed he'd felt back home. That first Monday, still wobbly from the flight, he'd walked easily to the Moskva Hotel, a great block of fake chrome and smoked glass. A room had been booked, as Ivanov had promised. The clerk told him a table had been reserved in the restaurant for twelve o'clock. Dimitriy went to his room, unpacked the few belongings he had brought, then turned on the television and watched a programme without really following it. What was Ivanov going to offer him, he wondered?

The Admiral was sitting at their table when Dimitriy came down, a vodka in front of him and a cigarette on his lower lip. He nodded curtly.

"Welcome to Astra," he said. "A drink?"

"Thank you," said Dimitriy, "but I don't drink at lunchtime."

Ivanov beckoned a waiter over.

"Today, you'll make an exception."

When the waiter had brought their drinks, Ivanov raised his glass. He had ordered caviar, brought by another waiter on a bed of ice. "Eat," he insisted gruffly.

"Thank you," said Dimitriy.

"Thank Mother Russia," said Ivanov, stubbing out his cigarette.

They started to eat, digging out the glutinous eggs with small mother-of-pearl teaspoons.

"What do you know about Tunguska?" the Admiral asked.

"Siberia? The beginning of the last century?"

Ivanov nodded. "30 June 1908," he said.

"I remember the pictures," said Dimitriy. "All those felled trees. A meteor, right?"

"Da, da," said Ivanov. "That's what people think."

"Think? What was it, then?"

"We don't know." He lit another cigarette. "I've brought a file for you to read, but before that, I want you to sign this."

Ivanov tugged an envelope from his jacket pocket and drew out a folded sheet of paper. "Official Secrets Act," said the Admiral, unfolding the sheet. "I will only tell you more if you sign. To be clear, if you sign the declaration and do not respect it, you could be tried and imprisoned. Not even your wife. Got it?"

Dimitriy read the declaration, his hand trembling. He would have liked to talk to Anastasia. Suddenly, she seemed very far away. He read it again.

"I need to think about it," he said. "I need to talk to my wife."

Ivanov shook his head grimly. "It's now or never," he said.

Dimitriy sighed and thought about the money. With such a salary they could easily rent a three-bedroom apartment. He was sure Anastasia would have agreed. She would surely have wanted to know what work the Admiral was offering. He signed and dated the paper and handed it back.

"Good," said Ivanov, putting it back in his pocket. He gestured to a waiter to clear their table and ordered two more vodkas.

"The Tunguska region wasn't as sparsely populated as people think," said the Admiral. "Quite a few people heard and saw something." He lit a cigarette. "It started with noises from the sky."

"Noises?"

"Da. You'll read the transcripts. Some of the witnesses said it was like trumpets."

"Heavenly trumpets?" said Dimitriy ironically.

Ivanov sneered.

"The noises went on for about a week," he continued.

"Then?" asked Dimitriy.

"There was some sort of *conflict*, in the sky," said Ivanov. "Some sort of *celestial* conflict."

"'Celestial'? You seem to be choosing your words with care, Admiral."

Ivanov stubbed out his cigarette.

"You'll read the file and see for yourself. As good scientists, we try always to keep open minds."

"The word 'conflict'," said Dimitriy, "suggests that more than one body or object might have been involved, right? And the word 'celestial' suggests this was high up?"

"There are drawings in the file," the Admiral said, "based on contemporary eyewitness accounts. The locals, the Evenki, were convinced they'd seen their god, Ogdy, in a fight."

"Fascinating," said Dimitriy, "but I am not sure why this should bring me to the Volga Basin and the Official Secrets Act."

Ivanov lit another cigarette.

"Leonid Kulik," he said. "A mineralogist. He came to Tunguska several times, starting in 1921. That was already thirteen years after the event. There was no crater — that puzzled him. How could there have been a meteorite impact if there were no crater, and if there were no fragments? He realised the fragments might have blasted out craters that had then got filled in. So, he kept digging holes to try and find filled-in craters with remains of one sort or another at the bottom — something, anything. No joy. Until 1938. His last expedition. One of his men found something, deep down, in a pit. Whatever it was, it blinded the man. He complained of an intense, searing light, then he lost his sight. Kulik's workers mutinied. For them it was proof they were messing with Ogdy. They dragged the man out and refused to get into the pit. Kulik had to shovel most of the earth back in himself. He measured the location as accurately as he could, and then returned to the Mineralogical Museum in Leningrad. He planned to return with his own men, but the Germans invaded in 1941 and he joined the fighting. The next year he died of typhus in a POW camp."

Ivanov drank some vodka.

"Whatever they found," he continued, "remained lost in the archives. For a long time, as you know, the motherland had more important things to think about than primitive superstitions. But in 2007 a group of archivists started going through Kulik's papers. When they got to the file about the 1938 incident, the team had the good idea of involving us."

"Us?" said Dimitriy.

"The security services," Ivanov said. "If another expedition to Tunguska were to be launched, they knew they'd need state resources. They dressed it up as being about some potentially weaponizable force. They weren't entirely wrong. Kulik's coordinates were accurate. They used a remote-controlled digger. Once they'd reached the depth Kulik recorded, they lowered animals down to the bottom. All came back blind. So, they were at the right place. A remote camera relayed images of glittering metallic fragments. They sent down instruments, but the instruments measured nothing. A volunteer discovered that *reflections* of the fragments could be observed in a mirror. Using remote cameras and mirrors, the fragments were dug out of the pit bottom. It was all hit-and-miss. Somebody thought of lead, being a heavy metal, so they fashioned a lead-lined steel box and used a remote-controlled robotic arm to shepherd the fragments towards the box and seal the lid."

"Shepherd?"

"You'll learn about that," Ivanov said; "*if* you take the job." He stubbed out his cigarette, drank off his vodka, and continued. "The fragments were then brought to a ..." (he coughed) "... *facility* here in Astrakhan. The box was opened and the fragments were housed in a specially-constructed room. That, Dimitriy Semenov, is where you come in. We want to analyse the fragments. Test their qualities." He leaned over the table as if to share a confidence. "And perhaps," he said, "replicate them."

Dimitriy felt the thrill of scientific discovery and the repulsion of a lifelong pacifist. But curiosity gripped him strongest. If only he could tell Anastasia! He was sure she would have been just as fascinated.

The Admiral got to his feet.

"I will be waiting outside tomorrow morning at seven," he said, "and will take you to the facility."

Dimitriy watched as Ivanov threaded his way steadily through the tables. That word, *comrade*, again. When he had gone, Dimitriy picked up the file and hurried to his room.

The Admiral was waiting for him on the hotel's esplanade in a sleek black chauffeur-driven limousine. He was in his uniform, his gold brocaded cap on the seat beside him.

"Is this a Zil?" Dimitriy asked, getting into the tobacco-fugged interior.

"The 4104," said the Admiral. "The Navy is determined to keep them going until they fall to pieces."

He lit a cigarette. "You read the file?" he asked.

"Of course. Do you want me to believe that the Evenki saw angels?"

"*You* saw the drawings," said Ivanov. "*I* don't want you to believe anything."

"Yes," said Dimitriy, "I *saw* the drawings."

The Admiral gazed through the smoked glass window.

"Do you believe in angels, Dimitriy Semenov?"

"No," said Dimitriy, "I don't. But what else can be made of those drawings? And those sounds; if not something like trumpets, then what?"

Ivanov shook his head.

"I told you; we are trying to keep open minds. You have to remember in 1908 the Evenki were a primitive, superstitious people. When something they didn't understand happened, they naturally ascribed it to their god, Ogdy."

"You don't think there was a conflict?"

"Imagine if you were a primitive people and something massive exploded overhead," said Ivanov. "Wouldn't you extrapolate from what you knew? Battle, noise?"

"And those trumpeting noises *before*?" asked Dimitriy.

Ivanov chuckled.

"*You* called them 'heavenly trumpets', Dimitriy Semenov, but you don't believe in such things, do you?"

"Of course not, Admiral. But what are the alternative explanations?"

Ivanov tutted. "You are a scientist, aren't you? Because we don't know the answer doesn't mean there isn't one. We just don't know it yet — perhaps we'll never know it. What we *do* know is that we have seven fragments of an unknown powerful material that *may* have fallen from the sky about the time of the Tunguska event. We can, and must, try to know as much about those fragments as possible, using scientific methods, and not basing our judgements on superstition and hearsay and eye-witness accounts from long ago."

"Of course," said Dimitriy, chastened. "It's those pictures in the file. My imagination ran away with me."

The Admiral stubbed out his cigarette.

"We have arrived," he said.

Some five months after Dimitriy started the job, Anastasia stopped making dinner on Friday evenings. The first time, she told him she'd been feeling unwell, and he accepted the explanation unthinkingly. He ate alone in the kitchen. The next Friday, though, the new practice had been rationalised; she said it was too late in the evening to eat a full-blown meal — better that he snacked or had a bowl of soup or a salad. He again accepted the explanation. Then, one Friday, when he came to bed, he found her weeping.

"What's the matter, Ana?"

She rolled over and he saw that her eyes were puffed up.

"I just wish you'd tell me," she said. "About her, whoever she is."

"There is no her," Dimitriy insisted.

"You can't hide it from me," Anastasia said. "I see the way you look as though you have been torn away from someone."

"There is no other woman, Anastasia."

"Is it a man? I'd understand."

"There's nobody else, I swear!"

"You think I'm stupid? You can't wait to get back on Monday mornings."

She rolled away and wept herself to sleep. He stared up at the ceiling. She was right, of course. The weekends back home in Derbent had become a torment.

"Welcome to Astrakhan State Technology University," said Ivanov, checking his cap's position in the glass of the chauffeur's partition.

The Admiral led him through the glass-fronted entrance. Students milled about, seemingly unfazed at the image of a uniformed Admiral threading a path through the crowd.

"Where are we going?"

"The Institute of Oil and Gas." Ivanov led the way across the leafy campus to a nondescript red brick construction. They went through rotating doors and stopped before a block of lifts. When the lift came, the Admiral pushed the button for –2, but he kept his finger on the button a long time. Ivanov turned to face a small camera in one corner of the roof of the lift and gave a salute.

"Forgive the cloak-and-dagger stuff," he said. "Until the Union collapsed, the Caspian Flotilla was based in Baku, but a lot of the command structure was kept safely within Russia itself, including here, in Astra. The Americans knew that, of course. This place was just as much of a target, so special underground facilities were built for the command structures. That's where we are going now."

By then, the lift should have reached – 2 level, but felt as though it were still in motion. After several minutes of slow movement, the lift stopped, and the doors slid open. In front of them stood two armed, uniformed guards. Behind them was a vast, brightly lit space. Ivanov produced papers and explained about Dimitriy. Once the papers had been stamped, the soldiers stood aside and let them pass.

"It's quite a hike," said the Admiral.

The vast space was devoid of human activity, but all around them stood massive columns of plastic-wrapped material.

"Thousands of men could live down here for years," said Ivanov.

On the far side of the bunker, Ivanov led Dimitriy into a complex of smaller spaces. Each entrance was a double-doored air-pressurized port. Finally, they came to a twin set of grey-painted heavy steel doors that had been swung open.

"Here we are," said the Admiral. "The playroom; the laboratory."

They were greeted by the head of the scientific team, Fyodor Babikov, a beanpole of a man wearing large tinted spectacles. Ivanov left them together, promising to return at the end of the day. Babikov showed Dimitriy to the changing room. There were sinks, lockers and benches. They scrubbed up together, then dressed in classic surgical gear. Afterwards, Babikov led Dimitriy into a small meeting room. The walls were lined with large drawings showing distinctive geometrical structures. Babikov gestured for him to sit down at a table and sat opposite.

"What has Admiral Ivanov told you?" he asked.

"The basic story," said Dimitriy. "And I've read the file."

"Did he tell you about their effects?"

"The blindness?"

"Well, there *is* that," said Babikov. "But you don't need to worry. The lab is rigged so that you simply cannot look directly at the fragments. You can only see them indirectly by using the mirrors we've installed, or by using the camera. But did Ivanov not talk about anything else?"

"Nothing," said Dimitriy.

"Mmm… He was probably afraid he'd scare you off."

"Why would I be scared?"

"They seem to have an addictively euphoric effect on some people."

"Some?"

"It seems to depend. There's nothing chemical about it."

"How do you know this?"

"You're not the first expert drafted in. In fact, you are the third."

"The others?"

Babikov shook his head.

"They didn't last very long. The first was here for just over a year. The second lasted almost two years."

"Where are they now?"

"Locked away," said Babikov.

"And you?"

"Nothing," said Babikov. "But, then, I don't spend hours in the viewing room."

"All right," Dimitriy said. "What else did Ivanov *not* tell me?"

"There isn't a whole lot more to know."

"How long have the fragments been here?"

"Since 2008."

"And you have honestly learned nothing?"

Babikov grinned.

"Honestly, very little. I'll tell you everything we know, but it won't take long."

Dimitriy leaned back in his chair.

"Tell me," he said.

"We know they have properties, and powers. The power to blind people, for example."

"Are we sure of that?"

"You mean?"

"Well," said Dimitriy, "we've only had that one example, of the man down the pit, back in 1938. It could have been a stroke, couldn't it?"

"You're forgetting the animals," Babikov said. "Anyway, there have been quite a few unfortunate episodes since."

"Here?" asked Dimitriy.

"Yes," said Babikov. "People who didn't listen. People who didn't believe. An accident. A drunk."

"How many?"

"Enough for us to know that the fragments, if looked at directly, cause blindness in humans, as in animals. Even welding masks didn't help."

"You've tried reptiles?"

"Oh, yes," said Babikov. "We've tried reptiles *and* squid and octopus *and* insects. We've tried everything," he said. "The fragments have the same effect on any sort of eye known to us."

"Your instruments?"

"Show nothing. Whatever this effect is, it is produced in an undetectable way."

"What else?" Dimitriy asked.

"Oh, the euphoria business."

"Can you be sure of that?"

"Scientifically, no. But there must be a strong presumption."

"Two cases only? You can't presume anything from that."

"You are right," Babikov said, smiling ruefully. "Let me just call it a *hunch*, then. Two highly intelligent, balanced, reasonable scientists, both following a similar pattern of obsessiveness and increasingly frequent episodes of manic euphoria, culminating in madness and confinement in clinics. I agree with you, Dimitriy Semenov. It could be sheer coincidence, but I think not."

"All right," said Dimitriy. "What else?"

"We have found a way to manipulate the fragments," said Babikov. "Only one metal may touch them — gold. All others melt away as they get near. Once we realised that, we had special gold implements made up that could be attached to the arms of the robots — that is the main way in which you will be working with the fragments, if you need to manipulate them."

"But it is curious," said Dimitriy, "gold being so malleable — like the lead in which they were encased."

"In retrospect, the lead-lined box was a crazy risk," said Babikov. "Who knows what might have happened if they had melted their way out during the trip?"

"What else?"

Babikov shook his head in sudden exhaustion.

"We know next to nothing, and that is all we know."

"Now you are talking in riddles."

Babikov looked at Dimitriy for a few moments, as though brought back from a reverie.

"We cannot record images. Nothing works; film, X-rays, electro-magnetic resonance imaging, transmission electron tomography... Whatever sort of imaging we have tried to use, nothing shows up. They are definitely there; we can see their reflection, but we can't capture them as images, and that means that we can only study the fragments themselves."

"What about microscopes?" asked Dimitriy.

"Lenses work," said Babikov. "But you cannot record what you are seeing."

"You can't draw them?"

"No, no," said Babikov. "They can be drawn, at least — hence all of these..." he waved at the drawings hanging on the walls around them. "Your predecessors' masterpieces."

"May I?" Dimitriy asked.

Babikov nodded.

Dimitriy studied the drawings for a while.

"I have an idea," he said. "But I'll wait until you've finished."

"Second," Babikov continued, "they are constantly levitating."

Dimitriy raised his eyebrows.

"They always hover, never touching any surface."

"Some sort of energy, then?"

"I think so, but we can detect nothing. We thought of magnetism or light but it's neither of those." Babikov smiled and shook his head. "Believe me, Dimitriy Semenov, we have tried and tested many ideas — all fruitlessly — so far."

"I understand what Ivanov was getting at now."

"Getting at?" said Babikov.

"We were talking about scientific method. He said we don't know the answer yet, and perhaps we never will."

That very first time Dimitriy came back from Astrakhan she'd known already, he realised — or, rather, she'd suspected already. Something had happened. He couldn't entirely hide it from her. For a start, there was the fait accompli of his decision. He had taken the job without first discussing the offer with her. It was so generous, he said, that he had decided on the spot. That wasn't the whole truth, of course. She asked about the work. He told her how he'd had to sign a declaration and was now bound by the Official Secrets Act. He saw her recoil.

"It isn't what you think," he'd said.

"What is it, then?" she'd asked.

"Something unimaginable," he'd replied.

She'd wrinkled her nose. "Can't you give me a clue?"

He'd laughed. "I promise you it's nothing sinister."

"I can see you are enthusiastic about it."

"Come with me to Astrakhan, Ana," he'd urged. "Bring the children. We can make it work."

"We discussed all that," she'd said, shaking her head. "My job, my family, the children's schools…"

He'd nodded his head slowly. Already, his thoughts were drifting back…

"Dimitriy?"

"I'm sorry, my love," he said. "I was daydreaming."

He'd listened patiently as Babikov listed the other properties his team had so far noted. The seven fragments were identical in appearance. Each was a convex oblong, about nine centimetres long by five centimetres wide. From a distance, they seemed to be golden in colour but, the stronger the magnification, the less colour there was. From very close up they seemed neither transparent nor invisible, and completely colourless yet iridescent. The fragments' default position was to hover vertically in an overlapping formation, like the defensive *testudo*

Roman legionaries had sometimes adopted with their shields. If the fragments were separated, they immediately moved back to the *testudo* formation. Once again, Dimitriy studied the drawings on the walls.

"So, what's this big idea of yours?" said Babikov.

"*Lepidoptera*," said Dimitriy.

"Butterflies?" said Babikov, momentarily confused. "We'd thought of fish scales, but *lepidoptera*?"

"In appearance they seem similar to fish scales, it is true, but butterfly scales have three-dimensional lattices that cause iridescence, and I just wonder whether some similar effect is not at work with these scales — and they *are* scales, Babikov, aren't they? They're not just fragments."

Babikov blushed. He took off his glasses and polished the lenses.

"Ivanov doesn't like such talk. I think he's right. We shouldn't leap ahead of ourselves."

"But are we?" said Dimitriy. "We know — or we assume — that these fragments fell to earth in June 1908, right?"

Babikov shook his head.

"No," he said. "We know only that they were found in the area where that event occurred."

"Ivanov gave me to understand there was a probability."

"So there may be," said Babikov. "But he doesn't want us to start wandering off into anthropomorphism and zoomorphism and all the rest of it. We know only what we know. The rest is speculation. If the Admiral hadn't given you the file, you wouldn't have started thinking along these lines."

Dimitriy smiled.

"What lines, Fyodor Babikov? What lines are those?"

Babikov remained silent.

"All right," said Dimitriy. "I'm sure you have similar thoughts. These so-called fragments are themselves a fragment that fell off something much larger, probably during that 'event' of 1908 — off a wing, maybe?"

"Enough!" said Babikov, waving his hands in front of him.

But somehow, Dimitriy *knew*; the fragments *belonged* to something.

In February, just over a year after his first visit to Astrakhan, Anastasia put the ultimatum to him. He couldn't blame her. The Christmas period had been disastrous. Derbent was bitterly cold and the streets were littered with filthy snow and slush where the gritters had passed. The morning, midday, and evening howls of the Ekranoplan as it departed and returned punctuated Derbent's days just as accurately and regularly as a clock tower bell. He couldn't wait to get back to Astra. He was constantly irritable with the children and mostly morosely silent with her. He felt dreadful. He needed to be back, to be back with *them*, in their presence. When the holidays were finally over, and he had been leaving for the Ekranoplan, she had said, "I can't say I'm sorry to see you go, Dimitriy. You have to get a grip on yourself. Whatever is going on in Astrakhan, you have to put a stop to it. It is ruining you and us."

That had been January. He had got worse over the following month. Then, one Friday evening in late February, she took the final initiative. Part of him felt she was absolutely right — he felt sorry for her and for Andrei and Sasha. But another part of him just didn't care. Or, rather, it only cared about *them*, the angelic fragments (which was what he called them now), and about being with them.

The children were in bed. The classical music radio channel was on. She'd even put a lit candle on the laid dinner table. It was the first time in a long time that she had cooked a meal for his return. At the end of the meal, Anastasia took his hands across the table.

"I am so very sorry, Dima," she said, "but I can't take this anymore."

"What do you mean?" he blustered.

She smiled and put a finger to his lips to hush him.

"You know what I mean. I have spoken to you so many times."

She was right.

"So, now what?" he asked.

"I'd like you to resign from your job in Astrakhan."

"But how would we..." he began, blustering again.

She shook her head and smiled wistfully.

"We were fine before. We'll be fine again."

"But my work is important."

"I'm sure it is, Dimitriy but, please, let somebody else do it."

He burst into tears.

"I can't," he wept. "I just can't."

"What do you mean? What is it that has such a hold over you? If it is not a mistress, then what is it? Drugs? Is that it? You can tell me. Please."

"It's none of those," he blurted. "But I can't tell you."

"Of course you can!"

"I have signed the Official Secrets Act, Ana."

"I promise I won't tell anybody else. Who could I tell, anyway?"

Dimitriy shook his head.

"If you won't tell me," said Anastasia, her tone hardening, "that's it."

"What do you mean?"

"I'll leave you, Dimitriy."

His shoulders sagged.

"All right, I'll tell you," he said finally.

He told her about his second meeting with Ivanov, and the file about the 1908 Tunguska event and Kulik's 1938 discovery. He told her about his first entry into the thick-walled, steel-shuttered underground space where the plate glass and mirrors had been set up to enable scientists to gaze indirectly on the fragments. He told her about his indescribable feelings of ecstasy, of euphoria, when he was in the presence of the angelic scales, and how the obsessive feeling had grown until it had now overwhelmed all other considerations. He told her about the steel shutter inside the space housing the scales which Babikov had to operate every day so that Dimitriy could at least no longer gaze upon the angelic fragments, and the way he, Dimitriy, had to be dragged out of the space by orderlies and given sedation before he could be convinced to return to his hotel room in the evenings.

Anastasia sat patiently through his explanation.

"All right," she said when he had finished. "Suppose everything you've told me is true. Where do you think this will all end?"

"I have to finish my work," he said. "Nobody understands the fragments better than I do. I have a *feeling* for them, don't you see? I understand them; their need to return. You see?"

She looked at him with sad eyes. "Of course I do, Dima," she said, "but you need to take a break. You're working yourself crazy."

"I can't take a break, don't you understand? I *must* continue."

"Nobody would blame you for taking a break," she said.

"But the *work*," Dimitriy insisted. "I *must* be there."

She shook her head. "No," she said. "You must stop this nonsense. You *can* stop it, you know. Let somebody else do it."

"NO!" he shouted, startling himself as much as Anastasia. "I can't let someone else come in. *I* must be with them. You can't stop me now." He broke off and wept. "Don't you see?" he said. "It's stronger than me."

Anastasia shook her head once more.

"You must choose," she said softly.

"No!" Dimitriy sobbed. "Please don't make me choose."

"If you go back to Astrakhan on Monday, then we will move out."

"But the children need their father!" Dimitriy blurted.

"Don't be a fool," Anastasia snapped. "The children haven't had a father for over a year now."

He nodded and hung his head. "All right,' he said. "Where will you go? Your parents?"

She nodded.

Good, thought Dimitriy, with a sense of wonderment at his own callousness. *Now I can go back to the fragments.*

Anastasia didn't come to the doorstep with him. He'd kissed her on the head as she lay in bed. She didn't move, though he sensed she was awake.

"Goodbye, Ana," he said. "I still love you, you know. And I'm sorry. I just have to be there."

He closed the door and walked through the slushy remains of the snow to the Ekranoport. He was petrified of the take-off, as usual, but his heart had already filled with joyful anticipation. As the Caspian Queen approached Astra, the sea became agitated and the sky darkened. A strong wind blew up and Dimitriy could feel that the pilot was struggling with the controls. He was relieved when the craft slowed down and started its long taxi up the relative calm of the Reka Bakhtemir channel. Ivanov was waiting for him on the quayside.

"Something's going on," he said. "We've been hearing noises in the sky."

"Heavenly trumpets?" said Dimitriy.

"Noises in the sky," Ivanov repeated. "But, yes, not unlike the descriptions the Evenki gave in 1908."

"Could it be?" asked Dimitriy.

"Be what?" said Ivanov, drawing on his cigarette. The sky flashed. A long roll of thunder sounded. "And we've been having strange weather. Look at those clouds."

Dimitry looked up at the dark, corrugated formation hanging heavy and low over the city. Thunder reverberated above and around them.

"And the fragments," Ivanov continued, "have started to oscillate."

"Oscillate?"

"All right," said the Admiral, flicking away his cigarette and blowing out smoke. "They seem to have become agitated."

"I can't wait to see them."

Ivanov gave him a sour stare then lit another cigarette and leaned against the Zil.

"I'm not sure that's a good idea, Dimitriy Semenov. They are no longer stable."

"What do you mean? I've got to see them. You know that."

"Pull yourself together," said the Admiral.

"It's just that I've *got* to see them. Surely you have understood that by now?"

The sky flashed and flickered. Ivanov looked up and waited for the roll of thunder.

"This is not normal," he said. "Something is going on."

"There's a connection?"

"I don't know, but I have a sense there might be. It's almost as though the scales are trying to escape."

"Ah! Escape?"

"Babikov says they have already melted through the gold lining on the roof of the cell."

"No!" said Dimitriy. "Then we must hurry. They are going back. I knew it!"

"Back?" Ivanov drew deeply on his cigarette. "Take my advice," he said. "Return to Derbent. The Ekranoplan will be leaving very soon. Go back to your wife and children. Maybe it's nothing. We'll see. Come again tomorrow."

"There's no point," said Dimitriy. "They've left me."

"Because of this?" Ivanov asked. "Because of your..."

"Yes," said Dimitriy.

Ivanov nodded slowly and drew again on his cigarette. They heard the distinctive whine as the Caspian Queen's jet engines started up.

"Go!" he urged.

"I can't!" Dimitriy sobbed. "I must see *them* again."

They leaned on a railing and watched as the gangplanks were drawn away and the aft and forward doors closed. The sky flashed vividly. A dockworker cast off the mooring ropes. When they had been entirely wound back on board, the jet engines roared, and the Caspian Queen sailed slowly out into the Volga. They heard the familiar howl as the captain increased the power and taxied the strange vessel down towards the sea channel.

Ivanov flicked away his cigarette, then opened the door of the Zil.

"We'd better hurry," he said.

"Ana," called her mother. "Come quickly."

Anastasia pulled the plug in the kitchen sink, wiped her hands on her apron and joined her parents in the living room. They were watching a Russian television channel and the news bulletin had just started. Sasha was playing on the floor. The newsreader was halfway through the headlines. A train had crashed just outside Vladivostok. The President had visited a new LPG facility at the port of Murmansk...

"What is it, mama?"

"Ssshhh," said her mother, "you'll see in a moment."

The newsreader finished the headlines. Anastasia's mother turned the volume up.

"And now we go back to our main news item this evening. Reports are coming in of a massive explosion on the northern outskirts of the city of Astrakhan, at the premises of the State Technology University. The explosion is said to have occurred in an underground research facility situated beneath the University's parkland.

"As can be seen from these helicopter images, several buildings have collapsed and the police and the fire services are searching the rubble. Among those missing are the director of the Caspian Flotilla's scientific outreach programme, Rear Admiral Anatoly Ivanov, and the head of the Astrakhan State Technology University's Oil and Gas Institute research programme, Fyodor Babikov. An acclaimed Moscow State University materials scientist, Dimitriy Semenov, who joined the research team from Derbent, is also missing."

Pictures of the three men flashed up on the screen for a few moments.

"That's Daddy," said Sasha.

Anastasia nodded tearfully.

"Yes, darling," she said.

"Babikov!" Dimitriy cried. He staggered out into the remains of the room where he had first met the scientist. He could hear flames flickering. The air was heavy with smoke. A long, low groan sounded out. "Babikov!" he said, "Is that you?" Dimitry staggered over to where he thought Babikov's office had once been. He heard the groan again. "Babikov?"

"Dimitriy Semenov," whispered the scientist. "What has happened to your eyes, man?"

Dimitriy smiled, the charred skin wrinkling where his eyes had once been.

"The fragments have gone back to their rightful place," he said. "I'm going home now."

*See Martin Westlake's story "Going Home"
online at Metaphorosis.
If you liked it, leave a comment. Authors love
that!
Remember to subscribe to our e-mail updates so
you'll know when new stories are posted.*

About the story

In the first place, 'Going Home' is drawn from, and is a conflation of, a number of lived experiences and/or curiosities that have fascinated me over the years.

- The strange tale of the Ekranoplan, developed in Soviet Russian times and then abandoned; https://www.youtube.com/watch?v=V8Nu94khHoo

- The howl of the Avro Vulcan bomber — once heard as a child and never forgotten; https://www.youtube.com/watch?v=w1igQoRqpBA

- The Tunguska event; https://en.wikipedia.org/wiki/Tunguska_event

- My personal acquaintance with Europe's last living Marial visionary, Gilberte Degeimbre, and the mixture of high euphoria and excruciating pain that she experienced and recounted to me — on the one hand, the joy of the visions, on the other, the pain of deprivation, once the visions had   stopped; https://en.wikipedia.org/wiki/Our_Lady_of_Beaur aing

- The account of an old Welsh miner I interviewed for a biography I was writing, who was dead scared of the trip down to the bottom of the pit in the 'cage' every morning but exulted in the camaraderie he experienced once he got down there. I wove into this mixture the tale of a man's addiction to his work, to the neglect of his family — a reality I have witnessed many times in my professional life.

The rest was imagination!

A question for the author

Q: What's an idea you're dying to write but haven't, and why?

A: I am fascinated by the themes Stanislav Lem explored so intriguingly in 'contact' works such as *The Invincible* and *Solaris*. High intelligences that (pace Ted Chiang's "Story of Your Life") are unable to communicate. Ostensibly sophisticated animal life forms that turn out to be mechanical. Phenomena that cannot be understood — at least not on human terms. I have been developing an idea for a story about a gradual parasitic invasion/colonisation of Earth that humankind cannot comprehend because it is occurring on such a lengthy time scale as to be imperceptible or unremarked. By definition, that puts the story far beyond any normal literary narrative cycle (beyond the life spans of characters, for example), which is a big challenge.

About the author

Martin Westlake has followed parallel careers as a civil servant and as an academic and has lived, studied, and worked in the UK, Italy, France, and Belgium. The only thing he has ever always wanted to do is write creative fiction. Science fiction exercises a special, but not exclusive, attraction in that regard. For the past fifteen years he has been working seriously at it and he thinks maybe he is starting to get there.

martinwestlake.eu, @MartinWestlake

Sanctuary

Chris Cornetto

The sentry's voice carried from the tower, filling the courtyard below. "Someone's coming! Open the gate!"

Abby dropped her basket and raced up snow-dusted stairs to the palisade catwalk. She leaned from the wall, bracing against the chill to peer into the storm. She wasn't meant to be up here, but no one stopped her – a privilege of being the Patriarch's favorite.

Beneath her feet, the wall shuddered from the rumble of unseen machinery. With a groan of protest, the gate yawned open. The wind lulled. In the distance, a shadow formed in the swirling white, a ghost drawn from the veil.

"It's Orphiel," someone shouted, and the cry spread from voice to voice. "Seeker Orphiel returns!"

A second form appeared behind the first, staggering through the knee-deep snow. "Look!" Abby called down to the crowd. "He's not alone!"

Her heart raced. It was a Homecoming, the first in five years, the third in her life. Not only had Orphiel survived the wasteland, he had found lost kin among the savages – a new life for the city, with new blood for the revival of their race. It was cause for celebration, and, for one unfortunate, cause for despair.

But it wouldn't be her. With her golden eyes and perfect silver hair, with the spurs of bone protruding from her back, she was *necessary* – not just to Father, but for the rebirth of the world. It was a humbling thought.

Below, the Patriarch waded through his eager flock, shining in his golden raiment like the sun among stars. "What are you waiting for?" he thundered. "Greet them." At his command, the crowd dispersed to put on their finest clothes, to gather gifts for their new kin.

Abby came down from the wall and picked up her basket. She had no need to change, as all her clothes were fine, but they were hardly warm enough for standing on the palisade. She huddled in front of a thermal vent and hugged herself for warmth.

Salome came over to join her, likewise shivering. "You must be mad, going on the wall in your condition. It's freezing out there." Though her hair was more blonde than silver, her eyes were finest gold. She, too, had little reason to fear.

"My condition, nothing." As if she couldn't handle a little nausea. She wasn't even showing yet. "I'll be fine."

Salome arched an eyebrow. "Say that to the Patriarch, why don't you?"

Abby waved her off and joined the re-forming crowd. Her people lined the avenue, resplendent with their blazing torches and best attire. Though only a shadow of the seraphim hosts of old, the sight still made her ache with pride.

Sanctuary, the last spark of civilization in a shattered world. How nervous, how excited their new Returned must be.

Abby shut the door behind her. She bowed her head lower than humility required to hide the grinding of her teeth. "You sent for me, Father?"

She knew why she'd been summoned. In the week since Martina's Homecoming, not a thing had gone right. The woman's sulking had cast such a cloud over the festivities that Father ended them early – and because it was Abby's task to make the newcomer welcome, she'd been dogged by the cruel smirks of those eager to see her fall. Being the favorite had its perks, but it painted a target on her back.

The Patriarch set his cup on the table. He rose and stretched his twisted wings, deformed but magnificent, before hiding them beneath his cloak. "I did, Abigail. Come here, child."

Across from him, Seeker Orphiel remained seated, one hand on a bottle of sparkling blue glass. Abby tried not to stare, though she'd never seen its like.

The Patriarch inspected her. "You are well, I trust?" His pale blue eyes, a defect inherited from his mother, bored into her.

"Yes, Father. Thank you for asking." She tried to pretend his concern was for her, but she knew better. She envied the child inside her; the Patriarch's interest in *her* waned by the day. It was for that reason, to prove herself the dutiful daughter, she had volunteered to be Martina's keeper.

What a mistake that had been.

He waved his hand. "Good. I need you to deal with Miriam again. She's not adjusting well, and there is no place in Sanctuary for idleness."

"She doesn't like that name, Father. Perhaps if we let her keep–"

The Patriarch silenced her with a glare. "What, keep her old name? Invite the taint of the wasteland into our walls? Don't be impertinent, girl."

Abby trembled. She looked to Orphiel for support, but he refused to meet her gaze. Flush though he was with the Patriarch's favor, that most precious currency, he wouldn't squander any to help her. "I only thought–"

"No, you did *not* think. Question me again, and I'll send you with her to clean the light-harvesters." Though it was an idle threat, his cheeks flushed an angry crimson. "Now, can you manage this *simple* task before I give it to someone more capable?"

"Yes, Father," Abby stammered. She retreated to the door, and all but ran to the women's barracks. Why did she keep sticking up for the useless woman?

Barracks 46 was farthest from the Patriarch's manor, and its residents furthest from his grace. Abby knocked only briefly before throwing open the door. "Miriam? Are you in?"

"Don't call me that," came a blanket-muffled voice. "I hate that name."

Abby went to the woman's bunk and peeled back the covers. "I know, I'm sorry. I wasn't sure if anyone was listening." She sat on the bed and ran her fingers through Martina's hair – its gleaming silver sheen left no doubt how the Seeker had found her. Despite the dark rings around her eyes, she was an attractive young woman, at most three years Abby's elder.

Martina brushed Abby's hand away and climbed back under the blanket. "Here to send me to sweep the snowfields? Or has the almighty Patriarch decided which of his stock I'm to be bred to?"

There'd be no reasoning with her in this mood, so Abby tried a different tack. "Have you had breakfast yet?"

Even in her warmest coat and scarf, Abby shivered. The light-harvesters needed constant sweeping, and it hadn't been hard to find someone willing to trade duties with her. Most of the residents of Sanctuary dreaded leaving the safety of its walls, even the short distance to the solar field.

Abby kept a nervous eye on the wall. Those Seekers not scouring the waste acted as the Patriarch's eyes – and the firm hand of his law. He would not be pleased to find the bearer of his child outside the walls.

For that matter, it didn't please Abby to be there, either. She shivered and swept and waited for Martina to speak.

After twenty or so minutes, Martina broke the silence. "Why are you here?" she snapped.

Because you're a fool who doesn't understand the bounty you've been given, Abby wanted to shout. *Because you don't see the glory of Father's plan, or the honor of being part of it.*

And because, when I make you see reason, Father will notice me again, her heart whispered. *He'll appreciate me for myself, and not just this child inside me.*

But she said none of these things, and settled on a neutral remark. "Because the machinery needs light, to keep the city warm."

The woman rolled her eyes and stopped sweeping. "That's not what I mean. I've heard the rumors. You're carrying the Patriarch's child. There's no way he sent you to freeze out here."

Called out on her scheming, Abby flushed. "I... I thought you could use the company. I worry that you're unhappy here."

"Unhappy?" Martina snorted. "And you enjoy being cattle?"

Abby cocked her head. "Cattle?" It wasn't a word she knew.

Martina gave an exasperated sigh. "Livestock. Animals kept and bred for their labor."

So they were creatures from the wasteland? She'd always been fascinated by the outside world; as a child, she'd pestered old Seeker Malthus for stories of its terrors. "But is that so bad? To survive, we all must labor and breed."

"It's not that simple. I hate the way Old Hunchback orders everyone around like he's some kind of god."

"Don't call him that!" Abby snapped. The woman's endless sulking was bad enough, but she had no right to insult Father. "Besides, he's not a hunchback."

"Not a–"

Abby dropped her broom and took Miriam's hands, guiding them beneath her coat to the spurs on her shoulders. To where, if the god was willing, her son would have wings. "Don't you understand? He's our Father, the greatest of us all. He's the closest to a seraph the world has left!"

Martina's eyes went wide. "You're telling me seraphim are real?"

"Didn't Orphiel explain why you're special? Chosen?" How ignorant *was* she?

"I didn't take him seriously! I get that my hair's odd, but it's just a quirk, isn't it? I assumed the old man was eccentric, and fancied a certain look." She paused and chewed her lip. "He really has *wings*?"

How could a woman of the blood, who had seen the wasteland with her own eyes, not understand the urgency of Father's project? Only by the return of seraphim could the world be reborn from its ashes. "If you didn't believe Orphiel, why *did* you come to Sanctuary?"

Martina looked at her feet. "It was a place to run away. My husband was killed by bandits, my home burned to the ground. I came because I had nothing left."

Martina passed Abby another plate to dry. "Why do you call it the wasteland?" she whispered.

For several days, Abby had been swapping chores to keep Martina company – and so far, bless the god, the Patriarch hadn't noticed. The two had arrived at something of an understanding, in which Martina tried to fit in so long as Abby didn't rush her. Abby had even come to like the woman, a little, despite her irreverence toward Father. Their candid conversations had become her guilty pleasure.

"Because everything was destroyed in the Cataclysm. Wasn't it?"

"Well, yeah, more or less. But that was hundreds of years ago." Martina plunged her hands into the basin and scrubbed the next dish.

Abby wrung out her towel. She set it down and hoisted herself onto the counter. "So isn't it terrible out there? Plagues and hunger, poverty and war?" She had heard all about it from the Seekers. "Didn't you want to get away from it all?"

Martina stopped washing. "I... thought I did. But I was wrong. I miss my home."

Abby's jaw dropped. "Miss *the wasteland*?"

Martina chuckled, her mouth quirked in a hint of a smile. "Have you ever looked around you? *This* is the wasteland. Nothing but mountains and ice as far as the eye can see." She paused a moment, looking thoughtful. "You've never been *anywhere* else?"

To her surprise, Abby felt stung. She knew as well as anyone there was nowhere *worth* going, but the way the woman spoke... "I've been to the lower village," she blurted, though it made a poor boast. Most of her kin called it the Dungheap. "It's... not a nice place."

"I think I passed through it on the way here. Crude little village, tucked in a valley about a day's walk down the mountain?"

Abby nodded. "That's the one." *Crude* was kind; it was where rejects were sent to huddle in stone huts, to scrape the dirt until they starved. "The people there don't have much. When there's a Departure, I sneak them some fruit from the greenhouse."

"Departure?"

On the walls, the crystal-lights flickered and dimmed – a warning that curfew was approaching. Abby cursed and jumped from the counter, and the two began scrubbing at a furious pace. "It's the rule," she explained over the clatter of wet dishes. "Seven-score and four. That's Sanctuary's capacity. The seraphim built it as an outpost, not a city."

"But what do you mean by 'departure'?"

"Well, if the population grows, someone has to leave, right?" Abby shrugged and grabbed another dish. It was an uncomfortable topic. She didn't worry for herself, but Martina... "There'll be one soon."

Martina stared at her. "What, so now that I'm here, someone gets kicked out of Sanctuary? Thrown away like trash? That's awful."

Abby winced. Departure was slow execution by hunger and cold, but it was also how things had to be. So why did she feel so defensive? "We hold a feast to thank them. And we walk them all the way down to the village."

"Oh, how noble." Her voice dripped bitter sarcasm "So who's the lucky winner?"

While most departed were picked for their weak bloodline, some were chosen for holding... dissenting views. Despite Abby's efforts, the current odds were two to one on Martina. "My guess is Michel, the engineer's son." It wasn't quite a lie. With his thin blood, and without his mother's aptitude, he was certainly at risk.

"But why not let me go home? Then Michel could stay..."

And let all my work go to waste? It was a selfish thought, but Abby couldn't help it. Besides, without ample provisions, there was no way for Martina to survive the trip back to the wasteland.

The lights gave a final hum, dimmed, and went out. Abby struck flame to a lantern, and they put away the still-damp dishes. It was too late to finish drying them, but at least they were clean. "Help me with the basin?"

Together they lugged the washbin outside, careful not to slosh water on the ground. The outdoor vents shut off at night, and spilled water meant ice in the morning. They dumped the soapy water behind the building.

Abby went back inside for the lantern, though it was hardly necessary in the crisp starlight. She locked the mess hall behind her, already shivering in the biting cold. "Can I walk you back to your barracks?" she asked through chattering teeth.

Martina hugged herself and nodded. "Gods, I hate it here. So damned cold."

Abby leaned close to Martina for warmth, frost crunching beneath their feet. "It's not cold where you come from?" She'd always pictured the wasteland with a blanket of ice, its people huddled in rude huts to keep from freezing.

"Ha! I used to complain of the heat. Silly, right?"

Abby shook her head. Her scarf slipped loose, and the wind raked chill claws down her neck. "So there wasn't much snow there?"

"In Sunhome?" Martina arched an eyebrow. "Never. We got enough rain for the crops, more or less, but that's the worst of it. Most days, the skies were so clear you could see the cathedral from my parents' vineyard."

They reached Barracks 6, but curiosity made Abby linger. She squeezed her hands to coax warmth into numb fingers. "Cathedral?"

"Like a big temple. Imagine the Patriarch's manor, but ten times bigger, and a hundred times more beautiful. My father would take me there when we brought our wine to market."

Abby studied the woman's face, but saw no hint she was teasing. Could a wonder like that exist in the wasteland? "And what's wine?"

Martina paused, and, for the first time, actually laughed. "Gods, girl, don't you know anything? It's a drink, made from grapes, sunshine, and a little bit of heaven."

Despite the cold, Abby flushed. *Did* she know anything?

Abby set the basket on the table. Steam rose as she peeled back the cloth, filling the room with the scent of fresh biscuits. She arranged the Patriarch's breakfast on his platter, set out his fine cutlery, and stepped back to wait. The blue bottle sat on the table, corked and half empty.

Most days, Abby's stomach would rumble in anticipation of her own breakfast; today it churned. She leaned against the wall, shifting her weight from foot to foot.

Uncomfortable minutes passed, followed by more. Just before she caved in and ran outside to vomit, she heard the tread of the Patriarch descending the stairs – followed by another. She hurried to pull out his seat.

"I'll get that," Salome said, reaching it first. Her dress was disheveled, and her blonde hair in disarray.

What was *she* doing here?

The Patriarch tugged his robe over his shoulders, smoothing it as best his wings allowed. "That will be all, Salome. We appreciate your zeal to serve, but I must speak with daughter Abigail now." He placed a hand on her shoulder and steered her toward the door.

Salome turned and dropped a neat curtsey. "As you will, Father. Goodbye, sister Abigail." She gave a coy smile and waved, showing a flash of silver on her thumb – a new ring, in a pattern of woven vines. A treasure scavenged from the wasteland.

Abby gritted her teeth. She hadn't merely lost Father's affection. She'd been replaced.

The Patriarch ignored her while he ate. When finished, he wiped his mouth and waved her over. "Come, child. Let's have a look at you."

Though fuming inside, Abby obliged. He lifted her shirt to place a hand on her belly, as he often did, but today her flesh crawled at his touch. She thought of Martina's favorite name for him – *the old lecher*. It had a nasty sound that fit all too well.

"My son is well?"

Abby nodded. Always *his*, as if she were a mere vessel.

The Patriarch furrowed his brow. "And you wouldn't be risking him by staying out late? By going out in the cold after curfew?"

That traitor Salome must have whispered about her! Abby's irritation twisted into fear; she prayed they didn't know she'd been outside the wall. "I've been working on Mar... Miriam, as you asked, Father. I helped her wash up last night. I think she's coming around."

He arched an eyebrow, and his frown eased just a little. "Very well. But be more careful. This child is my triumph... maybe even my heir. Think how honored you'll be as his mother – and how *terrible* it will be if anything happens to him."

Abby tried to control her quaking knees; she knew precisely whom it would be terrible for. "Yes, Father. Will there be anything else?"

The Patriarch picked up his cup and gestured to the blue bottle. "A drink, if you would."

Abby turned away to hide her fear. She wrangled the cork until it twisted loose with a pop. As she poured the ruby liquid, she caught an aroma of fruit and flowers. "What is this, Father?"

The Patriarch drank it down. He lowered the cup and wiped crimson from his lip. "A barbarian novelty, brought home by Orphiel. It would not interest you."

"Yes, Father," she agreed, though he was very wrong. She could guess what it was, and it interested her very much.

When he finished with his meal, the Patriarch rose from his seat and put on his gold-trimmed coat. "You may continue your work with Miriam, but I suggest you act quickly. I've put off this Departure long enough. It's time her faith was tested." Without waiting for a reply, he went outside.

Abby cleaned up from the meal, placing the dirty utensils in her basket. Still piqued about Salome, she also took the wine.

The greenhouse was the largest building in Sanctuary, and also the warmest. The citrus-scented air hummed with the drone of vents and honeybees. It was Abby's favorite place in all her tiny world, and the best in which to shake a bitter mood.

Martina spread her arms and closed her eyes. "I can almost pretend I'm home."

It had taken a few white lies to get Martina on greenhouse duty with her, but it was worth it. It was also less risky than leaving the walls with Salome snooping on them. "Is your home really so lovely?"

"All this and more. We have orchards that stretch as far as the eye can see, and the fruit... What I'd give to taste it again."

After checking that no one saw her, Abby twisted an orange from the nearest tree. "So now we're alone, will you tell me what's bothering you?" She peeled the fruit hastily, hiding the rind in her basket.

Martina breathed a heavy sigh. "I've been trying to take your advice, trying to keep my head down and make myself useful. But I don't know if I can go through with this."

Abby handed her half of the orange. "Go through with what?"

"I've been assigned to Orphiel. I found out this morning." She bit into the fruit and crinkled her nose. "Ugh, sour."

Abby tasted her own half; it was the same as any orange she'd eaten. "What's so bad about Orphiel? He's passing handsome." He didn't have the best traits, of course, but a Seeker had to blend with the savages. He had also become quite influential, as his acquisition of Martina had placed him high in Father's esteem.

"It's not that." Martina tossed the rest of her orange – a waste so extravagant, Abby couldn't believe it.

"That's *fruit!*" she whispered harshly. She picked it up and brushed off the dirt. "We shouldn't even be eating it!"

"Huh. Sorry." Martina gave a sheepish frown. "I guess I wasn't thinking. Back home, a small, sour orange like that wouldn't have sold for half a copper."

The more Abby heard of the wasteland, the less it sounded like one. "So what's the problem with Orphiel?"

"I don't like him. Those weeks on the road, between Sunhome and here, he barely talked. Just watched me like a hungry wolf. I was almost surprised he didn't try to... Well, I guess now's his chance."

"If you don't like him, why'd you come with him?" She ate a segment of the dirty orange. There was no sense wasting it.

"I wasn't thinking. My grief was so fresh, so intense, all I could think of was fleeing my ruined life. By the time I wanted to turn back, we were too far from the world I knew. I was afraid of him, but I was more afraid to cross the wilderness alone."

Abby squeezed her friend's arm; Martina's troubles made her jealousy of Salome seem a petty thing. Thinking of her rival brought to mind her stolen prize. "Oh, I know what might cheer you! I brought you something." She dug the blue bottle out from her basket and held it up triumphantly.

Martina's eyes went wide. "And you told me you'd never heard of wine?"

Abby handed her the bottle. "I hadn't. I sort of... borrowed it from the Patriarch. The Seekers bring him things from the wasteland. Orphiel must have given him this."

As the woman looked the bottle over, her lips trembled. She closed her eyes.

Abby frowned, worried she'd done something wrong. "Don't you like it? Is it bad wine?"

"No," Martina said through gritted teeth. "It was a kind gesture, and it's very good wine. It's just... a painful memory. This is Sunhome wine, from the Vianello vineyards. Bertholo had been saving a bottle of the same vintage for when... for when..."

The woman broke into tears, and Abby hugged her close. "Oh, dear..." Not knowing what to do, she patted her back.

"I was going to be a mother," Martina whispered through sobs, "but I lost the baby. I'm so sorry, Berto."

Abby squeezed the woman. She could imagine the Patriarch's wrath if she failed to carry her own child to term, and her muscles clenched in sympathetic terror. "I'm so sorry. Your Patriarch must have been furious."

Martina stopped sniffling and looked up at her. "We don't have a damned Patriarch," she snapped.

Abby drew back, startled. "So there's no one in charge? Everyone does whatever they want?"

"It's not that." Martina shook her head and rubbed her puffy eyes. "There are laws, sure, and the abbot expects his tithes, but it's nothing like here. There's no one controlling every detail of your life – telling you what to think and who to love."

It still sounded like chaos to Abby. "Then who assigned you to have a child with Berto?"

Martina laughed through her tears, a sound absent of mirth. "What a pair we make. I should be the one to pity you. Don't you know anything of love? Of family? *I* chose Berto." She tugged at a leather thong around her neck. "We said our vows, traded rings, and pledged our lives to each other – not because we were ordered to by a nasty old fool, but because *we loved each other.*" At those words, the tears welling in her eyes again overflowed. "And now he's gone."

Abby had no idea what to say, so she held the woman's hands in silence. She had never imagined any way other than the Patriarch's. The idea of having no one to order her life was terrifying... but also strangely enticing.

"I can't stay here," Martina said at last. "I can endure the loneliness and drudgery, but I won't be part of that filthy lecher's breeding project. If the gods see fit to send me another child, it'll be on my terms, to be raised with love. Not enslaved and bred for stock." Her face twisted in disgust. "A child deserves better."

Abby placed a protective hand over her belly. What did *her* child deserve? "What will you do?"

"I don't know. Does it matter?" She threw her hands into the air. "I guess, next time I'm sent to the solar field, I'll run off."

"Don't be foolish," Abby gasped. It wasn't a plan; it was a quick, icy death.

"The Seekers would drag you back before you made it ten paces. And even if you could outrun them, you'd freeze after sundown!"

Martina slumped against a tree. "Why do you stay here? A woman can endure much, but what mother would wish this prison on her child?"

Again, Abby brought her hand to her belly; already it swelled with the life growing within. She took pride in her favored status, and her child would be greater still, but Martina wasn't wrong. Beyond the cruel whispers and resentful glares, the price of that favor was the constant, gnawing fear it would be withdrawn. Her son's life would be governed, from cradle to grave, by the whims of the Patriarch.

All her life, she'd drawn no distinction between servitude and survival; she assumed there was no other way. But what if she were wrong? If Martina spoke true, Sanctuary's walls didn't keep the wasteland out – they kept her people in, slaves to the Patriarch's will. Yet somewhere beyond them, down the mountain and across leagues of trackless wilderness, people lived *free*.

Her head spun with the implications. She could hardly imagine what freedom was like, or what one did with it. What would she change about her life if she could choose?

There was one thing.

"Where you come from," Abby whispered, "can mothers keep their children?" It was a guilty thought, unbecoming of her, but it tugged at her more with each passing week.

"You mean..." Martina's eyes flashed with sudden anger, and she forced her words through gritted teeth. "That settles it. I'm leaving this place, and *you're* coming with me."

The Underworks rumbled like a sleeping beast, making Abby's skin crawl. Even coming from the greenhouse, the heat of the dim, damp tunnel was unbearable. It was not a place she went by choice.

"You're mad," hissed the engineer. "I should report you to the Patriarch."

The threat held weight. It was what any sane person would do when asked to participate in rebellion, and what the

Abby of a few weeks ago would have done in her shoes.

But Martina had changed her. Abby was sick of the endless jockeying for Father's approval, of the bitter distrust it caused. It was a tense, lonely way to live. Only Martina seemed outside the game – which made her the only person in Sanctuary safe to call a friend. She couldn't let Martina down.

"You won't," Abby told the engineer. "We hunger for his love and fear his wrath, but you hate him as much as I do." She nearly shouted to be heard over the clank of metal, the whistling steam.

The engineer looked away but made no denial. "Perhaps I should report you anyway, just to see his pet fall from grace."

Abby thought of Salome and her ring, and she flushed with anger. She placed a hand on her belly. "*This* is his pet. I'm just its husk." She had never spoken those words aloud, as if her silence could deny them truth, but they were true, regardless. "So, will you help?"

The engineer looked at her, her ill-concealed hatred giving way to the sympathy of one outcast for another. Still she shook her head. "I can't. As much as it would please me for the girl to escape his grasp, I can't risk it."

Abby wrung her hands. "But what about your son?"

"Michel will be fine. Everyone knows Father's going to pick Miriam." The woman's brow wrinkled when she frowned, and her nut-brown hair was shot through with gray – the fast aging another sign of her thin blood. "If she wants out so badly, just wait for the Departure."

"I can't." Abby mopped the streamers of sweat from her face. How did the woman stand it here? "We need to smuggle out supplies, a lot of them. We're not staying at the lower village – we need them to reach the wasteland."

The engineer arched an eyebrow. "We? You're going with her?"

Abby nodded mutely. She didn't belong in Sanctuary. The only thing keeping her here was fear of the outside world, but with Martina as a guide...

"You're not mad, you're suicidal. Where will you go? How will you survive?" She shook her head in disbelief. "There's nothing out there."

"But there is." It wasn't just Martina's stories that convinced her – she had seen the evidence. "The Seekers bring home things we could never make here. There's got to be more to the world than we're told."

The engineer shrugged. "Maybe, but what does it matter? You know he'll hunt you, even to the edge of the world."

"That's why we need you to give us a head start. Think on it. Even if Miriam gets picked now, what happens when my son is born? Michel is still at risk." Though she had little choice, it felt wrong to exploit the woman's attachment to her son. She used to think it unnatural, but now, with a life growing inside her, she understood.

The engineer chewed her lip, hesitating. "I just need more time with him. Once he grasps the machines a little better, shows how useful he can be…"

It was Abby's turn to shake her head. "And you'll teach him in, what, a mere six months, what took you a lifetime of study?" She squeezed the woman's calloused hands. The machinery was ancient, older than the Patriarch, and it took a rare genius to keep it thrumming – a genius Michel didn't have. "Let me leave. More room in Sanctuary means more time for your son."

"But your death–"

"Will not be on your conscience. I choose this." She couldn't explain the feelings rising inside her, how living only to serve the Patriarch would never be enough. Martina had opened her eyes, and there was no closing them again. For herself and her baby, she had to risk the wasteland.

The engineer slumped against the wall, defeated. "Fine, damn you. Second bell after sunrise, to give you as much daylight as I can. But you'd better reach the lower village by nightfall. Mark my words – a storm's on the way."

Maybe the woman *did* get it. It had been so long since anyone called the engineer by anything but her function, Abby didn't even know her name.

In the distance behind them, the alarm bell clanged.

Abby and Martina dragged the sled onward, unable to see anything through the blinding fog. The damp air sapped the warmth from their skin and frosted their clothes.

As promised, at second bell the engineer had overheated the main boiler and jammed the manual shutdown. Crews spilled through the gate to drag sheets over the light-harvesters, cutting off power, while others scrambled to open the vents full-blast. Steam met snow, blanketing the mountain in the thickest fog Abby had ever seen.

It was through that fog that Abby stumbled. The deep snow grabbed at her legs, pulling her to the ground.

"Come on," Martina shouted, hauling her to her feet.

Though there was little risk of being heard through the chaos, Abby still cringed. "Where's the track? I don't see it."

"We've already lost it. Just keep the sun to your back until we clear the fog."

Abby brushed herself off. She searched the sky for a hint of brightness, a smudge of silver amongst the white, but it was hard to be sure of anything. They took their best guess, and together they tugged the sled back into motion.

As the minutes stretched into hours, the bell grew fainter and eventually ceased. Abby trudged onward, each step an act of will. She ached with the effort, her muscles freezing through the heavy Seeker coat, but she didn't dare rest. In the best weather, for one who knew the way, it was a day's walk to the lower village. At their current pace, they'd never reach it by nightfall.

The fog followed them down the slope, but after another half hour it began to thin. A few minutes later, the sunlight cut through the haze. Martina, too weary to curse, pointed south and frowned.

Abby saw what she meant. From a different spur, divided from theirs by a deep ravine, the track snaked into a chasm. It was the only way down from the high plateau, and they'd have to backtrack to reach it. Uphill.

There was no use complaining. In this icy void, words were nothing but frozen mist, meaningless against the lonely silence of the mountain. They yoked themselves to the sled and trudged back the way they came, plodding one weary foot before the other until time ceased to have meaning.

When they reached the chasm, the sun had already passed its peak. Gray, billowy clouds scudded in from the horizon, devouring the sky ahead. The wind howled a warning of the storm to come.

And from behind rang the mournful note of a hunting horn.

Abby looked over her shoulder. Beneath the lifting fog was every Seeker in Sanctuary, racing down the slope in snow-gliding shoes. She froze like a hunted hare.

Martina shook her by the shoulders. "Snap out of it! We have to run!"

Abby nodded, and they tugged the sled into the ravine.

The winding track slowed their progress to a crawl. In some places, drifts piled so high they had to dig their way past; in others, rocks jutted through the snow to trip feet and snag the sled's runners. They couldn't see their pursuers, but each blast of the horn drew closer than the last.

As they struggled on, the first flurries danced through the air like mocking sprites. The flakes clung to Abby's coat until it was white as a burial shroud. The storm had come early.

With so many miles left, trapped between one doom and another, there could be no escape. If they weren't captured, dragged back to the city in shame, they would freeze to death in the snow. At the thought of her warm bed, tucked snug in the embrace of Sanctuary's walls, Abby sank to her knees and cried. "I can't. We never should have run away."

Martina slapped her, hard. "What, you thought this would be easy? Pity yourself later. Now get to your feet and pull!"

The vicious sting brought a flush of warmth to Abby's frozen cheek. She rose mechanically and picked up the tether, pulling the sled with flagging strength while Martina pushed from behind. Each step became a stumble until she pulled on all fours, head down like a beast of burden.

Though Martina huffed for breath, the woman kept her focused with constant chatter. Abby closed her eyes and fled her body, lost in stories of bustling markets and shining palaces. Of a cathedral, light gleaming from glass of every color, towering above a sprawling city. Of acres of fruit trees, not trapped in a greenhouse, but spread across the hills, warm in the generous sun.

Could it all be true? Had the world, once fallen into ruin, grown back without the seraphim? And if so, why did the Patriarch keep them in ignorance? She was too weary to process it all.

After a time, the sled halted. When Abby looked up, her heart caught in her chest. Before her, the canyon opened to a panorama of the slopes below. Though the sky was now full gray, painting the snow to match, there was another color far, far in the distance.

In a little valley, sheltered from the weather and biting wind, was the brownish-green of grassy fields.

Behind her, Martina cried out in alarm.

Abby whirled around to see her grappling with a Seeker, trying to writhe free of his grasp. They fell, skidding down the slope, and the heavy sled careened after them.

Too late, Abby noticed the harness tangled about her shoulders. It jerked taut, ripping her from her feet and dragging her with it. She clawed at the ground, but the icy scree gave no purchase. The attempt sent her into a spin, tangling her worse in the grasping cord. She skidded along with no sense of direction, curled instinctively into a ball to protect her belly.

A rock caught her foot and whirled her about; another struck her head with the force of a hammer. Stars exploded across her vision, and the world went black.

Abby drifted from one nightmare to the next, until she found herself lying on her back in a dark and frozen hell. Large, feathery snowflakes settled on a face barely warm enough to melt them. Only the pain in her head suggested she was alive.

She couldn't see through the blackness, but felt the sled rumble beneath her, heard it hiss along the snow behind the crunch of footsteps. How much time had passed?

She tried to move, and panicked when she couldn't. She thrashed harder, felt her body shift. Thank the god – she wasn't paralyzed. As sensation returned to her numb limbs, she felt the cords binding her to the sled.

So that was it, the abrupt end to her ill-fated plan. She was captured, dragged home to face her people's scorn, her Father's wrath. As battered and helpless as she felt, it was almost a relief. Of course, whatever happened to her, it would be so much worse for...

"Where's Martina?" Abby gasped.

"Hush. The Seekers are close on our trail."

Martina?

Abby slipped in and out of delirium until she couldn't tell the waking world from dream. Had she and Martina really escaped? Where were they, even? She caught a slight gleam in the sky as the moon tried and failed to pierce the thick, gray clouds. The world was nothing but snow.

Some time later, the sled ground to a halt. The air held a hint of smoke, but how could that be?

"I'm sorry," Martina rasped. "This is as far as I can take you."

The cords holding Abby went slack, and she felt the woman's arms around her torso, hoisting her. Her head throbbed as if it would burst.

Something creaked, and a foul draft wafted over Abby. A deeper darkness swelled around her, but it was warmer now, and out of the snow.

Martina lowered her onto a soft, prickly floor. "I'm going to lead them away from here. I'm sorry there's no food to leave you. When your child comes, give him my love."

Footsteps rustled. Something creaked again, and the darkness grew complete.

Abby woke in the dark to a throbbing head. She itched all over, but when she moved to scratch, lightning shot through her aching skull. She gave up and clenched her teeth, trying to ignore the crawling sensation she could do nothing about.

She was in a dark, reeking room that stank hardly less than the composter. She was cold, too, but not frozen – which came as a surprise as the memories trickled back. Where was she? Where was Martina? Her brain said to panic, but her body was too sore and weary to comply. She shut her eyes, useless anyway in the black, and slipped into a fitful sleep.

The next time she woke, a faint seam of light traced the outline of a crude but heavy door. The wind whistled an eerie tune through the cracks. She fought through the pain and eased herself upright. "Martina?" she whispered.

Something rustled in the darkness.

Abby strained her eyes until the room slowly came into view. The walls were unmortared stone, piled thick, and the floor was heaped with chaff. The shadow in the corner shifted again.

"Martina," she croaked through a parched and swollen throat. "Wake up."

The shadow crept closer, accompanied by the dull clank of an iron bell. It stepped into the streamer of light that trickled through the door, and Abby recoiled in horror.

It was a four-legged demon from some nether hell, with curving horns, a tuft of beard, and soulless yellow eyes. She scuttled away until her back pressed against the far wall.

Hot breath puffed against Abby's neck, making her skin crawl. Slowly she turned, barely daring to look, dreading what she might see.

There she was, face to face with a second demon, with nowhere to flee. Abby crumpled to the floor, overcome with terror.

She didn't realize she was screaming until the door burst open.

A man barged in and leveled a hayfork at her chest. He had silver-white hair and a thick beard. In Sanctuary, few could grow beards, and none did willingly – save a Seeker on assignment.

"On your feet," he ordered. "Come where I can see you."

Abby's blood ran cold. "Where's Martina? What did you do with her?"

The hayfork dipped, and the man squinted into the shadows. "You okay there, girl? Looks like you took quite a knock to the head."

"You're not a Seeker?" Abby brushed her scalp and found it tender to the touch. Flecks of dried blood clung to her fingertips. "Where am I?"

The man stuck his fork into a pile of hay. He gave a low whistle. "I'll be. No wonder I didn't recognize you. You're from up the mountain." He nudged the snuffling demon back from her, and it fell to munching dry grass. "Let's get you into the house."

Suddenly, realization dawned. The beasts, the beard, the crude stone hut... She had reached the lower village. But how? The dim gray light caused her head to throb, making it hard to think.

The man held out a hand. "Come on. Breakfast is still in the pot. Warm up, eat, and then we'll talk."

Abby let the man help her to her feet. She followed, her legs trembling beneath her.

"So how far along are you?" the woman asked. Brown-eyed and raven-tressed, she hardly showed the blood at all. She bounced a child on her knee, a dark-haired baby boy.

Dressed in her shift and a borrowed coat, Abby dug into her second bowl of thin barley gruel. It had little flavor, and, if there was any scent, she couldn't smell it over the burning peat. Above the firepit, the kettle had been set aside to make room for her drying clothes. "Three months, I think. Is it so obvious?"

"A mother knows these things," she said with a wink.

A mother. In Sanctuary, her son would have been taken from her, her purpose served once he was born. But here in the wasteland…

"Another bowl?" offered the woman. Her face was lean with hunger.

"Oh, I couldn't," Abby protested. She *could*, but the woman hadn't eaten, and the pot was near empty. She nodded to the baby. "Is he your first?"

"Second," she said, but her lips drew tight. "Second to live, at least. My eldest, Tiri, is taking the goats to pasture." The baby drowsed, and she set him in the cradle.

Abby looked around the little cottage, with its dirt floor, its walls of mud-daubed stone. Wind gusted through the chinks, stirring the smoky air. "It must be a hard life here."

"It is," admitted the woman, "but we make the most of it. We have each other."

The door opened, admitting the chill air of a crisp morning. The man came in, shook the snow from his coat, and wrapped his arms around the woman.

"He's your... husband?" Abby asked, recalling Martina's word for Bertholo.

"Aye," she said, "and I his wife. I hear they do things differently up the mountain?"

Abby nodded.

The woman took her husband's coat and hung it by the fire. "It must be a hard life there, too."

Abby had pitied the lower villagers for so long, the woman's sympathy caught her off guard. "In a different way, perhaps. But yes."

"It must be," the man said, "for you to have run away. Feel any better?"

"I do, thank you. But I came here with a friend. Have you seen her?"

The man and woman looked at each other, concern etched on their faces. It was the man who spoke. "A party from up the mountain passed through here during the night, and returned not long before dawn. I don't know if they caught her or gave up in the storm."

He didn't add the third possibility – that they had found Martina in no state to bring home. Abby prayed to the god that she was somehow safe, somehow still alive, but the prospects were bleak. "What if she's hurt? I need to find her!" Or at least find what happened to her.

The woman turned to her husband. "You'd best go with the lass. Let me worry about the fields until you're back."

The man nodded and draped his still-damp coat over his shoulders. "Alright, just don't overdo it. I'll hurry back."

Abby wrung her hands. "I could never ask that of you…"

The woman smiled, her eyes sparkling with tiny flecks of gold. "There's no need to ask."

There was no thought, no hesitation. Their generosity shamed her. "How do I thank you?" she whispered, trying not to cry. "I don't even know your names."

"I'm Davyn," the man said, "and the wife's Tarah. And think nothing of it."

But she couldn't. Overwhelmed by their kindness, Abby did cry. They had taken her in, given her food they couldn't spare, even though they had nothing.

No, not nothing, she realized. Abby saw with envy how the woman leaned against her husband, their child squirming in the cradle. They had something worth more than the safety of Sanctuary's thick walls and steady rations. They had a family.

Despite the snowfall, it wasn't hard to follow the Seekers' tracks. There had been eight, maybe ten of them in the group. It wouldn't surprise Abby if Father had emptied the city of Seekers to hunt her down.

As the sun rose, lighting the sky like frozen fire, Abby paused to lean against a stunted tree. She fumbled with the pouch of dried leaves Tarah had given her – featherfoil, the woman had called it. She didn't like the herb's bitter taste, and wondered if her nausea wasn't a little worse this morning, but at least it took the edge off her aches.

Davyn climbed a rock to peer above the thicket, searching the landscape with a frown. "It can't be far now. Not if they went this way."

When, a few minutes later, they broke free of the short, scrubby brush, Abby saw what he meant. The land fell away in a cliff so sudden it made her stomach lurch.

"Careful. It gets slick here." Davyn caught her elbow and steered her away from the edge. "Looks like they turned right, toward Giant's Nose."

A sudden gust tugged at Abby, yanking her coat and scarf, and she clung to the man who, a few hours ago, had been a stranger. Even in daylight, the track along the rim was daunting; she could hardly imagine how terrible it had been for Martina, alone in the dark. Where had her friend gone? "Is there a path down, ahead?" she shouted over the wind.

Davyn didn't answer. They marched on, crunching the snow's icy crust beneath their feet. A hawk wheeled and screamed; from far away, another returned the cry.

The path came to a headland, jutting over the valley below. The tracks formed a cul-de-sac in the snow, where the group had milled around before turning back. There was no way down – none that a person could survive. Had they cornered Martina here and captured her? Or...

Abby crept to the edge and peered over, her heart thudding in her chest. A cry escaped her lips.

Far, far below was the sled, dashed to pieces on the cruel rocks. Beside it were two bodies. Except for the blood, they looked like broken dolls, discarded by a careless child. She drew back in horror.

Davyn closed his eyes. His jaw clenched, and he swallowed hard. "I'm sorry for your friend. I'd feared the worst, but it's something else to *know*."

Abby sunk to the ground, numb with shock. The bitter wind pulled back her hood, teased her hair into streamers, but she barely felt it. She had abandoned her people and failed her only friend. Save the child in her belly, she was utterly alone.

Davyn took off his hat and twisted it in his hands. "Listen... Why don't you come back to the house? We can–"

"I have to see her." She wasn't sure why, but she did. She wanted to say farewell, maybe build a cairn. Martina deserved better than to be left for the carrion beasts. "How do I get down?"

The man gave a heavy sigh. "There's a rope we use to haul up peat from the valley, but it's not safe for a person. The wind could dash you against the cliff."

She'd given up safety when she left the stout walls of Sanctuary. She could skulk home once Martina was buried, but not before. "I'll risk it."

They backtracked half a mile, to where a rope was coiled beneath the snow – one end secured to a boulder, the other tied to a wooden basin. Abby stood in the bucket and gripped the rope for dear life as the man lowered her down. Though it swayed and rocked with every gust, she reached the bottom without disaster.

From there, she followed the cliff wall, climbing across shifting piles of scree. She nearly stumbled over the bodies before she saw them.

Up close, she recognized the other corpse. Joriel. He was the youngest Seeker, barely more than a boy, and eager to prove himself. She realized he was the one who'd caught them on the mountain slope, and the puzzle pieces shifted into place.

For a second time, Joriel must have rushed ahead of the pack. He'd caught Martina at the ledge, and, rather than be dragged back to Sanctuary, she'd flung them both to their death.

Had the other Seekers, mistaking Joriel for her, given her up for dead? What if that were why they'd turned around? It could take them a day or more to recognize their error, time she could use to get a head start... But to where? She had lost her friend, her guide. How would she survive the wilderness alone? Abby knelt beside Martina's broken body and wept, sobbing useless apologies.

Through her tears, she noticed something clutched in the dead woman's hand. It was a leather thong, torn from around her neck. Abby pulled it free of her grip, and stared at the mystery dangling from the cord – a silver ring, in a pattern of woven vines. Salome's ring.

Why would Martina have stolen it? When had she even had the chance?

Abby held the ring up to the light, awed by the workmanship. It had to be from the wasteland. The smiths of Sanctuary were adept at forging tools, but they brought no art, no beauty to their work.

It was also smaller than she expected.

On a hunch, she tried it on for size. Though Salome had worn the ring on her thumb, it was too tight for Abby's. She found it snug on her third finger.

There was no way Salome's hands were so tiny; the ring wasn't hers, but its twin. So what did it mean that there were two? What was she missing?

As Abby studied Martina's face, almost peaceful in death, her friend's words came back like an echo. *We said our vows, traded rings, and pledged our lives to each other.* Understanding struck her like a bolt from the sky.

It was no coincidence that Orphiel had found Martina just as her life had been destroyed. To persuade her to come to Sanctuary, he had first needed to isolate her. Bertholo's ring, the bottle of wine – they were a boast, grim trophies of the hunt.

Orphiel had killed a man, and for what?

She knew the answer. It was the same thing that drove all her people, had driven her. Father's approval.

Abby turned aside and retched.

Even in service of the cause, how could a Seeker do such evil? Did Father know the cost of his prize?

Deep, deep down, beneath the thoughts she allowed herself to think, she knew the answer. The great cause justified anything, even atrocity. Father would stop at nothing to breed seraphim back into this ruined world, because that was the only way to save it. The Seekers, as extensions of his will, would do the same.

Martina, her, her son... they were nothing but tools to be used and discarded. But what if the Patriarch were wrong? What if the world didn't need seraphim? What if all his plans, all his schemes, were nothing but the crazed obsession of a wicked old man?

There was only one way to learn the truth.

They left the next day, in the pale gray before dawn. Davyn led a goat laden with supplies gathered from around the village, while Abby followed. Everyone had chipped in.

Abby didn't question the villagers' kindness anymore. It made sense now. For people with nothing but each other, working together was a matter of survival, a way of life.

Together they cut through a small, scrubby forest, more brush than trees, until the village disappeared from sight.

The wind was fresh, and the sky brightened to liquid gold.

Some time after noon, footsore and hungry, they stopped for a quick rest. "Are you sure I can't persuade you to stay with us until the child comes?" Davyn offered. "Space is tight, but we'd make the room."

Abby scratched the goat's wooly beard. "I know you would. You've already done too much for me." She cringed to think what would happen if Father found them hiding her. And besides, she'd find no answers in the little village.

His mouth cocked into a half-grin. "Tarah made me promise to try."

By evening, they came to a jutting outcrop of rock. Davyn left the goat and scrambled to the top. "This is it," he called down to her. "The farthest I've been. It's guesswork from here."

Abby climbed up behind him and took in the view. The landscape rippled with shadow-dappled hills, endless steppe – and beyond that, who knew? She felt the walls of her tiny world expanding, giving her room to breathe. She sucked in the frosty air.

"Feels good, doesn't it?"

"It does," she agreed. The vast expanse, full of danger and possibility, thrilled her.

She was done being told how to live, what to believe. Never again would she be the Patriarch's creature – and god willing, her son never would be. Their choices, right or wrong, would be their own.

Abby closed her eyes and pictured Martina scaling the slope those few brief weeks ago – from freedom to prison, from life to death. She imagined herself treading those very steps in reverse, each footprint a guide and a gift.

"Thank you, Martina," she whispered to her absent friend. The words would never be enough.

See Chris Cornetto's story "Sanctuary" online at Metaphorosis.
If you liked it, leave a comment. Authors love that!
Remember to subscribe to our e-mail updates so you'll know when new stories are posted.

About the story

One reason I write short stories is to flesh out the world of the novels I one day hope to publish. "Sanctuary" began as an exploration of certain characters' roots (Abby's child among them), but it quickly became a philosophical exercise

To write this story, I had to consider how a totalitarian society controls its citizens. There are certain obvious techniques we see applied in countries that shall remain nameless: stripping citizens of identity, rewarding them for informing on each other, and forcing them to compete for the goodwill of the ruling class, just to name a few. It also doesn't hurt to have a caste of good, old-fashioned enforcers.

The true key to subjugating a population, however, lies in controlling the flow of information. It isn't fear of the Seekers that keeps Abby in Sanctuary, but her faith in the Patriarch's lies. Without an outside perspective, she lacks the means to question her society — until Martina's arrival causes cracks in her worldview. Only by having the courage to allow that *her* truth might not be *the* truth does Abby win her freedom.

For us as well as Abby, perspective is essential to freedom. When we allow others to curate our access to information, we surrender that freedom.

A question for the author

Q: Q: What's a typical writing day like for you?

A: It used to be a matter of taking my wife and our laptops to a coffee shop for the evening, but the lockdown put an end to that practice. I still find that, in order to focus, I require a space away from the distractions of everyday life. Therefore, my wife and I still go on our evening writing dates — we just brew our coffee at home and take it outside to the tent on our porch.

About the author

Chris Cornetto is a physics teacher by day and writer by night. In addition to physics, he has degrees in chemistry, philosophy, and psychology. He likes exploring ethical questions through fantasy settings, and enjoys long walks with small dogs.

Siberia in Four Dimensions

Esem Junior

Physicist Boris K. is one of three men held responsible for the catastrophic failure of Russia's largest supercollider, a classified, subterranean loop running 260 kilometers through Siberia. The underground explosion has left frenetic scribbles on Western seismographs and cost the Russian government trillions in rubles. It has also left one worker debilitated. This twenty-six-year-old man, perforated by subatomic particles traveling near the speed of light, lies on a cot in a metal Quonset hut. One half of his body has prematurely aged, now decades older than the other.

Anna adjusts her nurse's cap and watches Boris lean over the man. Huddled together within the small reach of a space heater, she sees what he sees: one eye bright, the other rheumy; one cheek baby smooth, the other spotted and furrowed. She touches her own cheek, wrinkled by many cold seasons.

The field hospital shudders under gales that clear all weakness from the larch forests at the 60th parallel. The patient is whispering and Boris leans in close. Anna hopes he won't notice the bulge under the patient's lower lip, where she's packed a boiled mash of iceland poppy seeds harvested from the boreal forest. Boris is Anna's son, but he is a creature of the state. For him, Moscow's medicines are always adequate. Russia never makes mistakes.

Boris lowers his ear close to the man's mouth. Anna knows what he's saying, because he's repeated it for days. "Time all at once, all at once."

Her son shakes his head. "Gibberish," he says. "What has he told you?"

Anna hesitates. She knows nothing of the supercollider — she's on a need-to-know basis and her post requires only that she tend to the ill. Her psychological profile report, however, never betrayed her talent for harvesting information. The sick man, under the influence of her gentle narcotics, has said other things.

"He said the stream pulled him in," she says. "What does that mean?"

Boris waves her off. "Impossible; he fell in. His own imbecility."

"Boris." Her voice comes from the back of her throat. "He lost his family."

The patient was beset by grief, Anna knows, after his wife and two children succumbed to pneumonia in this subarctic climate. She also knows that her son, when challenged, will speak without thinking.

But Boris only gives her a cold look.

"What stream?" she says.

"Enough," he says. His eyes narrow. Her son has the fortune of being a big man in Russia, and people rarely question him. Anna strangles her finger with a twist of gauze. She reminds herself that people like him put cosmonauts in orbit.

But the patient is mumbling something else.

Overhead, military personnel struggle to change the Quonset hut's camouflage netting to blend with the brown autumnal ground. The rustling interweaves with the man's whispers.

They step closer, to hear better.

"I see him," the man says, the hive of poppy seeds visible at his gumline.

Boris turns his head, apparently in disgust. "What?" he growls.

The man points a tremoring finger at Boris. "I see *you*. Alive, a hundred years more. Homeless."

Boris has had enough. He lifts the man by the hospital gown, but the gown is open in the back and the patient slumps back onto the cot.

Anna has no time to intervene. The door shudders, a blast of frigid air.

A soldier stands there, a middle-ranking officer with two yellow stars on his collar, chased by the smell of forest. The polish of his boots reflect the bars of hanging fluorescent lights. He is new, Anna notes. His footwear hasn't yet seen winter.

He surveys the scene, then looks to Boris. "What is the report?"

"The patient is unhelpful."

The soldier tut-tuts, but a smirk creeps into his jaw. "The eyes of Mother Russia are watching, comrade. It would be a shame," he says, "should history forget a man of your intellect."

Boris is a head taller than the man. Anna looks into her son's eyes and sees no fear. He has an intelligence quotient of 191, but sometimes she thinks fear might do him good.

Boris raises himself to full height and stands over the officer. "History will be kind to me, tiny lieutenant, because I will write it."

Outside, Boris finds himself surrounded by other Quonset huts — half-cylinders set on their sides, sheathed in corrugated steel. Green camouflage netting from the summer, piled on the ground, feathers under the winds. He has little patience for the military complex and its ant-like soldiers and their blind execution of orders. He is Russia's top physicist and the world's top investigator of the interplay between relativity and quantum mechanics, having mathematically proven the existence of twenty-four separate dimensions and having won the Copley Medal twice.

A man leans against the medical hut, slicing a crabapple. He has no uniform, no coding. His hair is long and waxed back.

"Tell me, friend," he says. His eyes are arctic, the color of a sled dog's. "Did the patient cause the implosion, or was it you?"

Boris eyes the stranger, then his knife. It's a Yakutian blade, forged by northern peoples for the purpose of skinning seals. He hasn't met this person, but he's met other versions, for the president's secret police are never far. Boris knows there'll be no logic to this discussion nor adherence to any rules, and this bothers him, more so than the military, because at least the Russian army has chains of command and order. Boris prefers equations with quantifiable results, efficiencies that can be measured. He distrusts the concept of rounding to whole numbers and the infirmities of human interaction.

The stranger's eyes crinkle. "You have a boy, yes?"

The worst thing, Boris knows, is to hesitate, to be soft. He might not understand all the rules of human etiquette, but he understands the most important ones. This rule he knows too:

that in Russia one is expendable until one makes oneself unexpendable.

"You," Boris says, "cannot decipher the terabytes left by the accelerator." He refers to the data recorded by the supercollider's sensors in the moments before the tunnel's implosion. A printout is kept in a subterranean vault. "Something extraordinary has happened. Half of a man cannot age unless there is a fundamental disruption in the fabric of spacetime. It is a new application of time dilation."

The man lifts a slice of crabapple with his knife and takes the fruit in his mouth. He cuts another slice, offers it to Boris. It's understood that, whether or not Boris accepts the fruit, something will be expected of him.

When Boris doesn't move, the man lets the apple slice drop to the ground. "You know nothing."

"I need the data."

"The first copy is free," he says. He chews with his mouth open. "The second comes for a price."

"You are obstructing something much greater than yourself."

The other man doesn't move.

"What do you want?"

"Something worth the weight of those papers."

In the next few hours, Boris's son will go missing.

Alexei sits in the old hunting cabin he shares with his family. His grandmother cuts his hair.

He loves these moments, their sounds, their scents. Anna spent her childhood here in Siberia, learning the land, and her kitchen steeps in the smells of the forest. She harvests its plants and secretes them into the cabin via hidden pockets sown into her dress. The acridity of cowberries, the must of lichen — these flavor their gruel from Moscow.

Each room is bugged with listening devices, but they cannot detect the rich aromas that suffuse her kitchen. Nor can they hear what Anna says because she taps her words in Morse Code on Alexei's shoulder.

"A man was hurt," she codes, while her other hand directs the barbers' shears. "He said a name — Planckatron." She is aware her grandson's friends have engineered a secret internet connection. "The name, you will look it up?"

Her touch worries Alexei. Her fingers move fast, some words are misspelled. But she's rightfully worried — something has happened, something to do with the recent earthquake. Since that moment, Alexei's father has changed. Less patience, more bark, even more bite. Under the shirt, where Alexei's grandmother touches him, a yellowing bruise matches the square shape of Boris' left fist. Each letter Anna drums into his shoulder leaves a dull ache.

Alexei recalls a time from before. Before Siberia, before his father was important.

This is the sum of his memory: an oligarch's estate outside Moscow, bearded men with suits but open collars, some in soldier uniforms. A stone mansion, a garden, and his father moving stiffly, a ship among icebergs. The children shooed away, Alexei among a group of boys who took turns killing birds with a slingshot. Then his refusal, their laughter, the heat in his cheeks — pizda, they called him. He walked deeper into the woods.

His father found him sleeping among leaves at the base of a hundred and fifty-year old oak tree, under the slant of autumn light. Boris lay down next to him and squeezed his hand. "Thank you son," he said, plum brandy on his breath, "for being here today. After today, we are no longer peasants."

Alexei had never realized they were peasants, and it was strange to hear the world imposed this architecture on them without him even knowing. His life until then had a been a collection of wonderful moments. Riding on his father's shoulder, reading with his grandmother by firelight. At the oligarch's estate that day he pondered this new dimension as they lay there, hand-in-hand, trading messages in Morse Code like Anna taught them, until the light weakened and the ground cooled.

Boris sat up. "Come, solnyshko, it is late."

Alexei resisted.

"Do not worry, son, this moment never changes." Boris looked up at the branches of the white oak. "The fourth dimension of time is like this tree. We are pushed through the trunk but, in every single second, we leave behind copies of ourselves. They remain imprinted there, like rings. Perhaps one day we can revisit them."

Alexei hasn't visited this memory for years and wonders if it resides anywhere in his father's memory. He guesses the answer is no and, now fifteen, he realizes this wasn't a good moment, but rather the sunset of something good.

His grandmother's scissors whisper in his ear.

She squeezes sentences into his aching shoulder, asking again about the internet search, and he encloses his hand over her fingers.

"Yes," he codes back. He'll do anything for her, no matter the risks. It was she who raised him, who told him bedtime stories about old Siberia that imprinted his mind with wonder. Stories about soldiers during the first great war who found the last living Neanderthals. Stories about her own grandfather, the first man to make an overland crossing to the North Pole. "He was a great man who did great things," she told him once, "and so will you."

They are interrupted. Boris shoulders through the door, a tome of paper tucked under his arm. He heads towards his study.

"Say hello to your son," Anna says.

"His mother's son." Boris walks as he speaks. "Unequipped for the real world, useless."

Alexei feels his grandmother's hand tense. He tells her, "Don't mind him, babushka. He is touched by Hans Asperger's disease." Russia has no such diagnoses for adults, but Alexei has read American articles online and wonders about this — Boris' obsessive focus, his abruptness with people. Russia abhors complicated labels — here, one is strong, weak, a genius, or a fool — but Alexei has begun to believe it's a world in need of further nuance.

Boris slams his paperwork on the table. He hoists Alexei from the chair by his collar. Only centimeters separate their chins, and spittle lands on Alexei's face as Boris yells. But Alexei isn't listening. He's happy. He has finally pulled Boris from the distant fugue where he spends his days, in some other plane of existence, and all Alexei wants to do is keep him here, keep him present in this moment.

"Enough!" Anna's palm smacks the table.

Boris drops his son, then points a finger at her. It is shaking. "You," he says. "You fill his head with garbage."

Boris is a big man, but Anna can steer him with pinches just above the elbow. She manipulates him into his study.

"What garbage?" Her words are crisp. This has nothing to do with her stories, she thinks, and everything to do with Alexei's comment. Boris is sensitive, and she wishes she could reassure him. He isn't handicapped, just incredibly selfish.

Boris grits his teeth. "Fairy tales, pseudo-science. You tell him the Red Army encountered Neanderthals during the great war. Nonsense."

"Your great-grandfather told me those stories. The same man who drove sled dogs over sea ice to reach the top of this planet." Anna remembers him sitting by a hearth full of fire, his eyes hazed with cataracts, telling her tales from his youth.

"Pradedushka wasn't the first to reach the north pole. The Americ —"

Anna holds her palm flat. She points to the lamp fixture, impregnated with a microphone. "That," she hisses, "is your blood. Show respect — for your ancestors, and the boy who comes after you."

"His mother's son."

Anna shakes her head. Alexei's mother was an Olympic-caliber gymnast, strong in will though small in size, her pelvis too narrow for childbirth. The Communist Party arranged this union, and Anna theorizes her son was enamored of the idea of marriage, of the idea of fatherhood. Never the reality. "It is you," she says, "who believes propaganda. Worse, lies of your own making."

Boris winces. He takes her wrist and begins to code. "I trade only in facts," he taps. "Here's one: we're in danger."

"Tell me."

He shakes his head. When they return to the kitchen, his papers are missing.

Anna throws the door open and steps into the winds. Their cabin is a hunting lodge that belonged to a twentieth-century tsar, and it sits at the edge of a village comprised of metal huts littered among the larch and pine. Their nearest neighbor, Mikhail, works beneath the monstrous undercarriage of a Burlak transport vehicle, each of its six tires taller than a person, all necessary to transport the Quonset residents to the government facilities located some miles north. Winter, after all, makes the roads otherwise impassable.

Anna has always liked Mikhail. He is handsome, soft-spoken, and were he born in the same generation her feelings about him might have progressed. She senses he admires her similarly.

"Mikhail," she says. "Have you seen our boy?"

He emerges from beneath the arctic transport vehicle shaking his head. "The children," he says, "lose themselves in the forest. I worry they wander into the Nikelgorod Exclusion Zone. When my own boy returns, we'll talk. So let us keep in touch, yes?"

Alexei treads the larch forest past the signs that warn of nuclear contamination. Beyond the trees, the abandoned, Soviet-era apartments of Nikelgorod rise against the sky. People are told this nickel-mining settlement fell victim to shifting winds after a seventy-megaton test. It's here that Alexei and his friends find solace, a private space of their own.

It is here that they climb.

Alexei finds the other boys at the base of a concrete statue of Alexander the Third, pioneer of the Trans-Siberian Railroad, rising twenty meters into the air. A military-style ushanka sits atop the tsar's head, while his hands rest on the hilt of a sabre, its pointy end touching the earth where the boys sit.

They huddle around a tablet, watching a Frenchman scale the Burj Khalifa in Dubai without rope. They watch for technique, to help them plot a route from where they sit to the top of Alexander's ushanka. They've grown bored with Nikelgorod's other structures — the theater, the church's onion dome, every façade of the nickel-processing plant.

One boy nods at Alexei. He lives in the Quonset hut closest to Alexei's cabin. "Are you ready to conquer Alexander the Third?" he asks. The boys bond over this preoccupation, not so much with each other, for at any moment the military may tear one of their families from this Siberian wasteland and post them in another dystopia. At nine thousand kilometers wide, Russia has many such places.

"A moment," Alexei says, and rounds the statue and takes a seat by the heel of the tsar's boot. He removes from his satchel Boris' paperwork.

Alexei has tried to make sense of his father's paper on the walk through the taiga but, without the internet, it's hopeless. He fishes from his pocket a chipped mobile phone — contraband from Outer Manchuria that musters no cellular signal — and connects to his friends' wi-fi hotspot. He must know what's so classified and unknowable about his father's life, why they live a half-day's drive from any city and near a government installation that appears on no map. For this, everything was sacrificed, and Alexei simultaneously feels the ache in his shoulder and the warmth of his father's hand behind the oligarch's estate. He wants to reclaim that moment and capture the alternate history that might've happened between them, but first he must know what led them astray. But can he possibly decipher his father's papers? Alexei doesn't understand physics. Not vectors, not forces, not relativity, much less the mathematic hieroglyphs that describe them. But as his internet browser loads, he rescans the papers, and something stands out. The top right corner of each page has numbers divided into angles, minutes, and seconds — GPS coordinates, the same ones the boys use to navigate the forests. Alexei thumbs these into his phone.

The coordinates form a massive circle, stretching north. The closest spot lies two hundred meters away, so Alexei slips away through an alley between the old theater and bakery.

He finds an empty field at the town's outskirts, but the grass here is newer, the conifers shorter, a superhighway of fresh vegetation that runs beneath his feet and stretches through the taiga. He wonders, how has he not noticed this?

The nearest building is a smooth, windowless cuboid, roughly the height of Alexander the Third. It's one of the few structures the boys haven't summitted. At its base stands a set of iron doors, impervious to crowbars. But there's a crack that zags up the side, having appeared after the recent earthquake, and he knows from summiting nearby buildings about the hatch on the roof.

At the building Alexei assesses the crack. He's the smallest of his peers but, with urban climbing, being small has its advantages. His hand fits into the fissure and, by making a fist, he can anchor himself to the wall. Using both hands and feet in this way, he can jam his way to the top. The boy puts on his climbing shoes, their rubber soft and sticky, throws on his backpack, and chalks his hands.

The inside of the crack bites against his fists — every move requires complete attention — and in this demand for presence he can climb from the fugue of insults and inhabit a moment existing outside the literal and proverbial reach of his wayward and adulterated father, outside the scramble of the world's confusion.

At the top, the crack continues from the side and across to the hatch, and has broken the trapdoor from its moorings. Alexei lifts the square of iron and descends down the awaiting ladder.

They take Boris six days later. Eventually they come for Anna.

It's the man without a uniform who questions her, accompanied by a soldier Anna knows from the field hospital. They sit at a table in the cabin's kitchen, where the man without uniform cleans his fingernails with a caviar fork. The soldier won't look at Anna, and she stares hard into his face, searching.

Anna and this solder have spent three years now at this military camp. He and his brethren have grown accustomed to her hospitality, her birch sap teas, her high-octane coffees. As she walks from the cabin to the field hospital each day, she alerts them when the tips of their noses whiten, a precursor to frostbite, and fixes their balaclavas to keep out the arctic cold. These soldiers are still boys, and miss their mothers on the far side of the Urals. Like boys, they cower before powerful men.

The soldier refuses eye contact while the other man continues to remove grime from his thumbnail with the caviar fork. Anna refuses to acknowledge it. She looks over this other man. The cracked leather of his jacket has the dull sheen of cockroach wings. He wears sunglasses with aqua lenses, like those preferred by aging rock stars. She asks, "Your mother has given you a name?"

The man smiles. "You may call me Volk."

"That is not a proper name."

Volk shrugs.

"What is your family name?"

"Family?" he says. "What does it matter, if their poor choices doom us? It's a thing of beauty to survive, grandmother, especially when the world conspires against this."

Anna appraises his sunglasses.

"You are blind?" she says.

Volk squints through the turquoise glass.

"Only two people wear sunglasses in basements, sir. Blind men, and fools."

The man laughs. "You," he wags a finger, "I like you."

Anna feels encouraged. "Speak to my son Boris, he is a big boy. Bigger than you."

"But it's the little boy that interests me. He has been missing quite some time now, no?"

Chilled blood washes through her ribcage, but Anna is quick. "Allow me to find him, then. Who better to lure him than his babushka?"

The man reaches out and touches the tines of the caviar fork to where her collarbones meet. "You say those lines. Soon you'll believe them."

Volk removes the caviar fork from her skin. She dares not look down at the two dimples that surely remain, the skin within their orbit pale and swollen.

"You have three days. After that, I cannot help you."

Anna is a tough woman, but she understands bad things happen to people in this country. She should know. For years she managed an infirmary in the basement of a Moscow federation building, wheeling victims on gurneys through dishwater-gray corridors, treating their cigarette burns, their naked fingernail beds, the stumps of missing toes.

"I'll see you on the third dawn," Volk says.

Later, Anna looks out a northern window at the soldier standing post, shuffling his feet so they don't freeze in his boots. Behind him, through a window in the neighbor's Quonset home, the neighbor's boy is watching too. In the condensation on the windowpane he writes something, then wipes it away.

It was too small for Anna to see.

At the ladder's end, Alexei finds a concrete hall awash in red light. The ladder meets the floor at a right angle but when he touches down and let's go of the rungs, his shoes slide across the floor towards its dark end, leaving tracks through a metallic film on the floor. He grabs the ladder. He is still young enough to believe in the impossible, to wonder at its mechanics, and for the first time he considers that his father's secret involves a truth more precious than any of them.

There are shelves on the walls, anchored with bolts, and hand-over-hand he lowers himself down the hall. The confusion of gravity dizzies him. Where the shelving runs out of length, the room opens into a chasm steeped in blackness. Alexei hooks an elbow around one of the shelves' uprights and removes a pocket flashlight and throws wattage into the hole.

The light is drawn to the center of a large space where a miniature planet hovers, a black planet rimmed in embered light, orbited by disks of the same colors. An evil tiny Saturn.

It pulls the luminescence from the flashlight and casts auroras against the walls, dancing as in a grotto, but this isn't a cave. It's a tunnel — an enormous tunnel, big enough for a subway and yet there are no tracks. He can put no name to this thing.

There is no echo in this space, no sound. It's as though Alexei's reached the end of all things, an edge of the universe.

He fumbles for Boris' papers in his backpack with his free hand. But the papers are thick, meant to be held with two hands, and the leaves split open and fall instantly, sideways, pulled toward the tunnel's center.

He shines his flashlight after the papers. They hover in the air a few meters into the larger space, oozing into the abyss. Their edges begin to curl.

The boy is nauseous, woozy. Hand-over-hand, he moves back toward the ladder and ascends it.

Outside, the world is different. He's loitered in the tunnel perhaps twenty minutes, but it is the night sky that greets him, and it twinkles over a layer of snow that blankets the buildings and treetops for as far as he can see. He thinks that whatever his father has been up to, it can change the universe, and he questions whether his ideas about life have been too small.

Anna boils water on the wood stove. The yellowing sky above the eastern tree line has begun to wash out the starlight. It's the third dawn.

For three days she's hiked the forest, looking for the boy, leaving ribbons on trees and cairns by streambeds, encoded with messages, but the taiga has offered nothing in return.

She unwraps gray, army-surplus toilet paper nearly to its cardboard core and removes the Wolfsbane she's pressed there. The flower's purple shade is still vibrant. The toxins reside in the roots, but she throws the entire plant in the bubbling water and sets out two cups, one for Volk, one for her. She'll drink first, while he watches, then offer him a cup. She re-enacts the scene until her breathing slows. She no longer has a reason to exist, the generations before her deceased, her son and grandson lost to cruelty.

When the knock sounds at the side door, she jumps.

It is Alexei.

She can only stare. He looks clean. He wears the same clothes as the day he disappeared — his olive canvas jacket, his blue ripstop nylon pants. His hair hasn't grown.

"Where have you been, boy?" She embraces him, envelopes him, their hearts beating just inches from one another. She can feel the muscles in his back; he's eaten well. From a part in his hair, she smells the autumnal foliage that disappeared from the forest with the first snow. "It's been six weeks," she says, and holds him away and studies him. His eyes have the shape of confusion.

"Six weeks?" His eyes flit around the cabin. "Where is dada?"

"Taken." Anna closes her eyes, takes a breath. "Taken north."

"To the circle?" He refers to Stalin's arctic death circle, home of Russia's modern gulags.

"His documents, they need them back. They are classified."

The boy stiffens, but there's no time for questions. A knock rattles the front door.

It is Volk.

He opens the door and removes his gloves. "Good morning, grandmother," he says. "You'll recall we have an appointment." Another man stands at his aft, holding a fifteen-centimeter Makarov pistol.

"Have you found —" But Volk doesn't finish. He sees the boy. "Ah," he says, "the prodigal son returns."

Anna taps words on her neck — words only the boy can read. They need more time, she writes.

Like his father, Alexei never hesitates. He turns to Volk and says, "I have your papers. In a cave, in the mountains."

"You'll take us there."

Anna clears her throat. "Tomorrow. He will take you tomorrow, what is another day? Give me one day with my grandson."

Volk rounds on the boy. "How far is it?"

"A hundred miles," he says.

Volk scans the boy's shoes. Athletic trainers, not boots. The man takes a loose cigarette from his shirt pocket and lights it. He puffs long enough to grow a red cherry at the tip, then turns the cigarette around and appears to contemplate its ember and its many, many uses. "You travel light."

"Gentlemen," Anna says. She steps toward the stove. "Let the adults have tea. I have just boiled water."

Volk puts a hand on her arm. "For everyone then. The boy too."

"It's not to his taste."

Volk smiles. He walks to the stove and looks into the boiling pot where the limp purple petals flutter in the rolling waters. He drops the lit cigarette into the pot.

"Okay, grandmother." He turns toward Anna. "One more day with your grandson."

An hour after they leave, the boy falls asleep in his bed. Awake or asleep, Anna feels blessed to spend these moments with him, watching his chest rise and fall. He looks the same as Boris did, when he was young, and she traces the contours of his face with her fingertip. She feels lucky to have another soul in this arctic world. It's all she has.

Boris' letters from prison, folded in her dress pocket, prod against her abdomen. Her mind skips to what he's written. "The boy, a victim of his own imbecility," in that chicken-scratch scrawl. "A fool." Anna dabs her eyes with a shirtsleeve. Boris is a man who cannot sew his own clothes nor cook his own meals. A selfish man, of the most selfish variety, focusing on his equations, desperate for the acclaim of his superiors, to the exclusion of all else. It was she who allowed him to devolve into such a creature. "It's my fault," she whispers. But she knows the past is unchangeable, that only the present is in play.

When the soldiers come at nightfall, she meets them at the door.

They pull Anna from the house.

"I need my winter coat," she says.

"This will just take a minute, babushka," one says.

They are strong, and the toes of her slippers drag against the crust of the snow. She steals a look at the neighbor's Quonset hut and sees the neighbor's boy, backlit in a window. She thinks of her own Alexei. He has no protector. She opens her mouth to cry out warning but the other soldier's hand is ready. Her scream dies in his glove.

Volk waits behind the cabin, finishing a cigarette. He drops it into the snow. "Grandmother, your wish was granted. But this is our way, you know this. There are no gifts in this country. Here we pay for everything."

The report of a single shot from a Makarov pistol sounds through the Siberian night.

Then another.

When the soldiers re-enter the cabin, Alexei is not in his room. He's not in the kitchen, nor in the bedroom, nor anywhere they know to find him.

"Your son has admitted to everything."

"Release me then," Boris says.

"You are his conspirator. Fellow saboteurs."

Boris sits back down in his cell. Through a narrow window he can view the arctic wasteland, when it's not obscured by snowstorms or sulfur dioxide emissions from the Norilsk mines. He curses his son. The narrative in his mind tells the story of a short-sighted boy, selfish and vulnerable to whim. Still, as much as Boris thinks he knows, his thoughts are infinite but bounded.

The first thing he doesn't know is that his bosses are in trouble, because to date nobody has explained what caused the supercollider's implosion. A loss of five trillion rubles isn't easily stomached. The second thing he doesn't know is that, in the tunnel's surviving segments, a layer of palladium, four microns thick, coats the walls. The price per gram of palladium is twice that of gold, and the president has demanded someone re-create this alchemy.

Russia's other physicists haven't been helpful.

Soldiers return Boris to the cabin, where he finds himself provisioned with a copy of the papers he lost and a mandate that he cannot leave the premises. The soldiers take away all his outerwear, even his shoes. Anna, meanwhile, is nowhere to be found, and nobody tells him why. The soldiers have simply said she'll be back, and he believes them.

Whatever questions he has end up suffocating in the focus he reserves for the supercollider data. He reads the papers far into the evening by candlelight, analyzing numbers and calculations. Only the wood stove provides warmth.

The palladium he can explain. The particle accelerator's last experiment smashed atoms of tin into one another, knocking off protons. With palladium sitting four spots left of tin on the periodic table, its creation makes sense. But other data doesn't. The equations cannot balance, even if Boris accounts for string theory's extra spatial dimensions. He can hear his mother's voice as though she were at his ear. "You have identified twenty-four dimensions in your work, but what about the dimensions of love? The dimensions of fatherhood?"

These questions are born of her letters. His photographic memory preserves every character of her looping script. "Get home," she wrote in the letters he received in the arctic prison. "Help me find Alexei. If I cannot appeal to your sense of decency, perhaps then your curiosity."

These words create a knot in his throat he cannot swallow away.

One night the weather is particularly foul, the insides of the windows frosted, the taiga beyond lost in whiteout. Boris is alone, unobserved, and he takes every article in the house and examines it.

The boy's shoes sit beneath the table, their treads caked with a silvery-white metal. Boris steps across the room to the hearth. In the back corner he's spotted the faint imprint of a small shoe in the ash. The interior stones of the hearth are layered in char and so he cannot spot the sticky black rubber left on their surfaces, these footsteps tracking up into the darkness.

A knock sounds at the door, but nobody waits for response. A soldier throws it open.

"Emergency!" the man barks. Behind him stands the neighbor, carrying his own son. The boy's sock is sticky with blood.

"Bandage him, be quick," the soldier says, giving the neighbor wide berth, his eyes skipping between the boy's bloody leg and his own spotless uniform. The neighbor, older than Boris by a decade, turns almost carelessly, swinging his son's leg, grazing the soldier's wool overcoat.

"Idiot!" The soldier checks his fabric, huffs, then steps out the door.

Boris turns to the neighbor. "I'm not a medic," he says. He suspects a compound fracture, bone through skin. "You've confused me with my mother."

The neighbor shakes his head. "I am not mistaken."

"Yes you —"

"We have no other choice. Please, have faith."

Faith, for Boris, is a dangerous word. It asks him to leap to conclusions without the bridge of data underfoot.

They lay the boy on the kitchen table. The soldier monitors through the milky rime on the windowpanes.

Anna's med-kit sits in a closet, below her hanging clothes. Boris sets water to boil and opens the kit, then takes trauma shears and cuts away the boy's sock. He sees nothing, only a mess of syrupy plasma, and he dabs a cloth into the pot of simmering water, then at the skin, clearing blood, trying to locate the wound.

He dabs the entire ankle and finds nothing, then looks at the boy's father. His name is Mikhail, Boris remembers now.

Mikhail removes his jacket. There is another jacket underneath, and he removes this too and throws both into a corner. From a shirt pocket he pulls a roll of cloth. "Use these bandages," he says. His eyes are burning. "Disinfect the laceration, set the fracture, wrap the ankle."

There's no fracture to set, but they pretend. The boy screams and the soldier squints through the frosted window. Boris pores iodine over the ankle, then unfurls the bandage around the joint.

"Cut here," Mikhail says.

Boris hesitates, and Mikhail's hand closes over his own and guides him to cut the bandage. The remnant fabric on the roll bears writing, and Mikhail tosses it into Anna's med-kit.

"My own boy, so foolish," Mikhail says. "Fooling around in Nikelgorod ... falling from buildings, exposed to radiation." He meets Boris' eye. "We must not give up on our foolish children."

"Your boy will be okay," Boris says. He is realizing something. This man, his mother — they are complex beings with complex thoughts, operating in dimensions unfamiliar to him.

He pulls Mikhail into an embrace, his lips a centimeter from the man's ear. "Radiation in Nikelgorod is a story," he whispers. "It keeps people away. Stories — wonderful things, yes?"

"When shared," the older man says.

The Siberian winter arrives, and the soldier guarding the cabin stands on the porch, his eyelashes heavy with frost. Boris hands him a cup of birch sap tea. It's all he can do not to break the porcelain cup on the man's teeth. The inscriptions on Mikhail's bandages contain stories — about the soldiers' habits, about what happened to Anna. He first decided he would kill those responsible — he doesn't know their names but he has their physical descriptions. They have taken something from him and his first instinct is to balance equations, here with revenge.

Fortunately Mikhail's bandages also hold a blueprint for moving forward, and this plan demands restraint.

Near midnight when the guards change shifts, Boris stirs a new pot of birch sap tea. He finds Anna's copy of Nabokov's *Invitation to a Beheading* and removes, from its final pages, the dried yellow toadflax that she's pressed there. The yellow flowers, brittle, disintegrate in the bubbling water and sigh the faint odor of wet dog. Boris hopes the birch sap will cover this smell. Sips from the tea will force a lengthy visit to the outhouse that stands frozen behind the cabin.

Contrary to popular belief, Boris has always paid attention, and his memory forgets nothing. So he knows all of Anna's herbal recipes and their pharmacological properties. He merely believed, once, these things were unimportant.

At midnight a new soldier knocks at the door. A blizzard has overtaken the night, the winter dust infesting the cup of tea that passes between the men.

Thirty minutes later, Boris watches the soldier run to the latrine.

They've taken Boris' goggles, his jacket, his boots. But he remembers his great-grandfather's stories about the Samoyed peoples in the far north, with slitted eyewear carved from driftwood that filtered the harshness of weather. Boris has cut a like slit in his belt, and fashions the leather around his head. From behind the wood stove he pulls out snowshoes fashioned from wool socks and floorboards. From a closet, Mikhail's second coat. From Anna's keepsake box, lastly, he removes his great-grandfather's steel Adrianov compass.

Boris opens the door to westerly purge winds, laden with ice chips, hazing the visible world from reckoning. He strikes out north in blowing weather that fills his footprints.

He feels what his pradedushka must've felt. Dizzied, no horizon, blundering through roiling clouds of pixelated white. He is proud — to walk in the footsteps of his people, to go beyond. His chest fills with this ancestral spirit and, barring an Act of God, he'll find the boy. He checks the Adrianov compass every forty steps to confirm his bearings.

At the faceless, oblong building in Nikelgorod, he finds Mikhail and his boy at the entrance. "My son believes your son came here," Mikhail said.

Boris punches numbers into a keypad and tumblers unclick. The door, thick like a bank vault, swings inward without sound.

Before they enter, Boris asks the boy, "How would my son get through here?"

Mikhail's son motions for the men to follow. He circles the building and points to the fissure that travels up into the whiteout. "He would've followed this."

Boris barely fits his palm into the crack. "Impossible," he says.

Mikhail lays a hand on Boris' shoulders and feels a slackness in Anna's son. He is surprised. The physicist is an imposing figure — there's always been a rigidity to his posture, in his very being — and Mikhail is encouraged to find plasticity in the man. He wants to do right by Anna, by her family. Mikhail is a mechanic who keeps the military's all-terrain vehicles in repair, with their monstrous tires and snow tracks. He believes he and Anna were the same, both grips in the play of life, moving scenery when others darkened the stage.

"Tonight," he tells Boris, "we triumph over impossibility." He prays for this. There is a cosmic debt he must pay, for he watched the soldiers drag Anna to her death from the dark maw of his kitchen and did nothing. His son, too, is in arrears. The boy never told what he knew about Alexei's disappearance — until the crack of midnight gunshots broke across the plateau.

Boris leads them down into building's gut and, at the bottom of a ladder, they find a concrete hall cast in submarine-red light. They grip the ladder, necessarily so, it seems. Mikhail feels as though if he let go, he'd fall across the room.

"This isn't right," he says.

He shines his flashlight across the floor. The palladium coating offers a soft luster, but Mikhail trains the beam along its surface and into the tunnel.

Alexei is suspended ten meters in, motionless, withdrawn into a fetal posture. His own flashlight points back, a deep-red circle. Beyond that, a black sphere of nothing hangs in the deadened space, silently orbited by an accretion disk, the swirling light warped as though twisted through a carnival mirror.

"My god," Mikhail's son says. The boy releases the ladder and begins sliding across the floor, palladium gathering in ribbons along the outsoles of his boots.

Boris grabs him.

"It's pulling me," the boy says.

"No," Boris says, "you're falling."

Mikhail has locked an arm around the ladder. "Falling? Into what?" He's dizzy, and cannot reconcile how one falls sideways.

"It is …" Boris shakes his head. He points light into the tunnel at various angles, tries to illuminate its center, but this isn't possible. Everything is swallowed. "A black hole."

Mikhail knows these are formed by dying stars in deep space. He's a maintenance man, not a cretin. "Impossible."

"For many reasons."

"Black holes are big. They cannot fit in tunnels."

"Comrade, black holes can be any size, if you press enough mass into a small enough area. Could we squeeze the earth into the skin of a gooseberry, we'd have such a thing."

Mikhail looks into the abyss, at the curled form of Alexei. He pulls his own boy close. "Why is he stuck there?"

Boris' voice is soft. "He's not stuck. He's moving fast, from his own perspective. Within milliseconds he'll be crushed, in his frame of reference."

"But he's right there." Mikhail points.

Boris sinks to the floor, scraping at the palladium with a thumbnail. "It's the black hole's gravity, its effect on time." Light, he explains, struggles to escape such a thing and yet light must always travel at lightspeed, regardless of circumstance. "This is Einstein's great contribution," Boris says. "If light must always travel at the same speed, and gravity retards its progress, then time must slow down. The seconds dilate so that light can catch up."

Mikhail finds the other man's voice distant, defaulting to the jargon of his trade. Perhaps comforted by it. "This is difficult for me," Mikhail says.

"You will see. Even with us, only seconds are passing, but for the world outside —" Boris motions up the ladder "— it is days, maybe weeks. Could they see us, we would look frozen too."

The maintenance man puts his hand on the physicist's neck and looks into his face.

"We will problem-solve, our people are good at this. Explain to me. Alexei is right there, just meters away."

The big man's eyes have teared. "There is more to the story, look at the red-shifting." He nods at the orb of Alexei's flashlight, a deep red and nearly invisible. "His light is just reaching our eyes, just as starlight from distant galaxies shows us what once was. We are looking into the past."

"If time has slowed," Mikhail says, "perhaps we can reverse it."

"Enough," Boris says. His jaw has tightened, his shoulders too. He wipes his eyes. "The boy is lost." His logical brain patterns have re-emerged. "Let us focus on what's here — the Solar System's only black hole."

Mikhail sees, reflected in the man's eyes, the red auroras that dance on the walls.

"We can be heroes," Boris says. "Each of us."

"But the boy."

Boris inhales. "We must judge objectively. Rescue is impossible."

It is Mikhail's turn to steel up. He feels Anna's breath gather in his lungs and his voice comes low but clear. "Let us have faith."

"But —"

"But nothing." Mikhail can see the line of saltwater that rims Boris' eyes. He can see that Anna's son is breaking down, succumbing to the physical laws of humanity, finding within himself emotions other than anger. "We will get back your boy."

It is summertime when they emerge from the building. Under weak cover of the season's two-hour nightfall, they approach the camp.

They find it deserted, bare as Nikelgorod.

Three days later, they have backed Mikhail's tow truck to the entrance to the oblong building and, with the help of his son, knotted the tow cable to a makeshift harness fashioned from steel chains. Boris yokes himself into these riggings.

Alexei tethers himself to the ladder with a retraced figure-eight knot, snaking the rope through his nylon mountaineering harness.

The tunnel's air is heavy and pressing; Alexei feels as though he's underwater at depth. The harness cuts into his legs and he packs himself into a ball. But he created the disorder, he thinks, and his mind drifts to the report of the pistol, dampened by the wall of spruce logs shielding that terrible thing from view. At that moment and for the first time, he felt as though he were nothing more than an assemblage of flesh and bone. A bloodless creature. But for his father, Alexei is alone in the world, completely and utterly, and to retrieve the man from the gulag, to restore the world he once knew, he must retrieve the papers. In this way can reverse the world's entropy.

The pages drift deeper as Alexei draws closer. No longer frozen, they continue to curl. The closest paper floats just a half-meter away.

This is when the rope snaps.

He looks up, toward the ladder, and swears he can see his father and the neighbors, just a blur of them, up and down the ladder, in and out of the cave, but over the course of a microsecond. There's little time to process because Alexei's in freefall, being crushed, unable to swell his chest to inflate his lungs.

But options appear.

There are frames before him, layers of time stacked, and he can see himself, copies of himself, lined up overhead. A proverbial flipbook of his life, and what Alexei finds is that he needn't fall further. He can move in the opposite direction, second-by-second in reverse, traveling back through time, and it starts by uncurling himself and reversing the choreography of his fall. With a backward dance through the air, the boy inches his way back towards the ladder, back towards home, rewinding his life. The rope unsnaps, his decision to leave the ladder undone.

Outside, he pauses in his reverse-scale down the oblong building. It's all there, the taiga's piney smells, the gritty surface of the crack against the back of his fist. He cannot do anything new but must backtrack through the passageway he's already etched through spacetime. Inhaling carbon dioxide, exhaling oxygen, but he's alive, somehow. Alexei surveys the top of the arboreal forest and savors the moment. He'll be able to see everything again.

When his gaze returns to his hands he finds a horsefly crawling backwards on his arm, something he hadn't noticed on the climb up, and he twitches his forearm.

The horsefly doesn't respond.

He understands then. His father talked about time as a fourth dimension, the trunk of a tree through which all matter moved, all past moments permanently inscribed in its rings. He flexes harder against the encasement of his life, beating notes against its paralyzing membrane.

It's not enough to merely visit the past, he realizes then. He wants to say all the things he wishes he'd said, do all the things he wishes he'd done.

Alexei knows that every action has an equal and opposite reaction and so he wonders, if beating against the wall of the fourth dimension won't affect his past moments, then what is he disturbing? If he can't affect the moments that make up here and now, then when?

Boris sinks toward the black hole. He shines a flashlight toward the ladder where Mikhail keeps watch; when clicked off, his neighbor will raise him back. The older man will be significantly older when Boris returns, the micro black hole placing them on different worldlines with different experiences of time. His mind returns to the patient with the ruined face, and Boris theorizes that the micro black hole, born of the supercollider, sped in its infancy through the tunnel and passed within inches of the victim's head, its core singularity fundamentally changing the fabric of spacetime for long enough to place each side of his face on two similarly different worldlines. It is this issue, he thinks, that truly merits his attention.

The big man mutters to himself. The idiocy of this plan, the romantic beliefs of modern-day peasants. How, he wonders, was he swept up in their mythology? But he swallows this down. He knows. He knows that without the reckless pursuits of his pradedushka, he wouldn't have known how to navigate the blizzard. Without the lessons of his mother, he could not have imprisoned the soldier in the outhouse. Without Mikhail's cunning he would not have learned the fate of his mother or the whereabouts of his son. He understands, now, the beauty of other people, their existence, the strength in their numbers. He wonders if this is love.

Spacetime squeezes Boris as he descends, funneling him toward the singularity. It has obsessed him, this micro black hole. By his calculations, it is a billion tons of mass compressed into the space of an amoeba. The weight of 107 billion people, the mass of each and every ancestor to all those persons currently alive.

He's made it about halfway to the boy and, as he predicted, Alexei falls deeper, in slow motion as his eyes shut and his mouth opens to scream.

Boris knew this would happen — that pursuing the boy would be a chase without closure, that moving nearer to Alexei would only speed up the moving picture of the boy's inevitable death. Einstein's models predicted such a thing, based on tested calculations, and Boris for once cannot stomach being right. What he didn't anticipate was the accelerated effects of time dilation on himself. He knew the world he's left behind would move in fast-forward, but his own calculations are flawed. As Boris sinks toward the dark singularity, Mikhail appears and disappears up and down the ladder, under the crimson glow of the lights, more quickly than anticipated. Ten times, twenty times, a hundred times, Mikhail is blipping in and out of sight, aging, then an old man, then gone.

Boris clicks off the flashlight.

He's alone, doomed, a speck in the universe. His son is gone, Anna is gone, Mikhail is gone, and no longer can he witness their impossible feats nor celebrate them as he should have done.

He thinks of Mikhail's trickery of the army, his son's fifty-foot ascent along little more than a fault line. All the science and medals in the world will not replace them. He tells himself these feelings are simply in his genetic hardwiring, in the hardwiring of all humans — social creatures engineered to feel this way for the sake of their collective survival, no different than pack animals. But he will surrender, there is no other way. In searching for memories of Anna, of his son as a baby, Boris finds he can't even remember their faces. Boris turns to look at his son, to reanimate the flashlight and shine its light on his face.

But the chains pull him back.

The neighbor's son greets him by the ladder. His hair is salted, his skin leathered. He's older now than Boris.

"What year is it?" Boris says.

The man tells him.

"You minded the truck so many decades?"

"I held two lives in my hand," he says. "How could I not?"

There is little left of the camp. The Quonset huts have rusted through, the roads cracked and weedgrown. There is only the hunting cabin, which Mikhail's son has maintained. Boris removes his two Copley Medals from their encasement in a glass frame and hands one to Mikhail's son and buries the other in the spot shown to him where Mikhail is buried. It's all he has to give. The two men embrace and Boris realizes he has not hugged anyone as an adult, not his mother, not his son. His body tenses, the weight of the other man against him, the smell of pine in his coat. He stays there in that moment.

Before the sun disappears he finds a familiar black poplar and walks forty paces north and unburies a box that contains money and his identification. The next day, in Novosibirsk, he waits for the train. The Trans-Siberian Railway has changed little, though a ticket to Moscow is quadruple what he remembers. In the capital he will inform the Kremlin of his discovery. He has nothing left now but his life's work and it will have to be enough.

On the steps of the Ministry of Defense along the Moskva River, police in mirrored visors intercept him. They ask for identification, they listen to him, they laugh at his story — a story only a homeless man could tell — then arrest him and throw him into the back of a utility vehicle. Boris finds himself among a half-dozen vagabonds, their shoulders and knees touching. They are driven to the outskirts of the city and into a forest, where the police tear them from the vehicle and push them to the earth. Boris finds himself alongside a buckled asphalt drive, disrupted by the roots of old-growth trees. Once the police van leaves, the other men trudge after it, presumably toward a highway, toward civilization. But for Boris, something is familiar about this road. He follows it in the opposite direction.

He comes upon a decayed estate and realizes he's been here before. It was here he had the greatest moment of his life, where the ruling party plucked him from the ranks of basement physicists and raised him up. By the hearth of a great room he stood with men of power in a circle, upholstered in cashmere suits and gold. Servants distributed Cuban cigars and copper mugs heavy with vodka. Boris knew, then, he was indispensable. So he'd thought. Because he had always been indispensable, he sees this now, but he never valued the smaller circle of souls who needed him.

He walks through the ruins of the estate. The autumnal breeze whines through the great room and the hearth is choked with dirt and the skulls of rodents, a forsaken den, a forsaken man walking through an apocalypse. It's as if the world Boris knew never existed, as if he never existed, and he recalls the insult of the tiny lieutenant who threatened such a thing, and the words of the young man disfigured by the supercollider who foresaw this very result. Boris stumbles through broken doors to the back of the estate, the lawn interrupted with yellow leaves. His feet guide him forward — he's taken these same steps before, though he can't remember where they lead.

Beyond the hedges he finds himself surrounded by birch trees and then a white oak, two hundred years old. Sunlight dapples the forest floor, a last kiss of warmth, and he sits among leaves of embered colors and lays there, his head against the earth.

His son.

He remembers, and the encasement around his heart cracks.

With closed eyes he can see the memory, the two of them at this very spot, both prone and side-by-side, hands clasped, trading code through the smallest pulses, a practice born of Anna.

Boris feels outside himself, heady and light, in third person, and he feels these palpitations again in the center of his hand.

Except this is not memory.

This is something new. Boris doesn't know how he knows this, but he knows it is Alexei. He can feel his son near — clouds of his gravitons interacting with his own through the fabric of spacetime, across dimensional membranes, beating letters on the surface of his palm.

"It is me, Alexei."

The message pulses, over and over, proof of dimensions beyond the twenty-four Boris has identified, a dimension of love that tethers distant moments in the fourth dimension. The small dark star in the underground of Siberia has amplified this interstitial gossamer, clarifying messages over an impossible difference. He thinks of megaphones in a crowd, fiber-optic braidings across the oceans' floors, of all those abysses throughout the history of the world where bridges have since arisen.

Boris' eyes well with saltwater. He knows so little, he can admit this now.

"I left you there," Boris squeezes back to his son. "I was too late."

Too late to be any good to him, too late to catch him in his fall, too late to realize that he'd viewed the world through a tiny keyhole and never once considered all that others had to teach him and all there was to really know.

"I failed," he signals, embracing that tiny hand in his, unseen but sentient.

"We are here now," the boy says.

See Esem Junior's story "Siberia in Four Dimensions" online at Metaphorosis.
If you liked it, leave a comment. Authors love that!
Remember to subscribe to our e-mail updates so you'll know when new stories are posted.

About the story

It only took me a couple decades since high school to revisit the theory of relativity and, once I absorbed it with a more fully formed brain, I couldn't stop thinking about it. Meanwhile, no discussion of relativity can take place without reference to black holes and, lost one evening in a Möbius Strip of internet links, I came across an article on a supercollider under construction in Europe. The Swiss community had come undone by the prospect that supercolliders, theoretically, could give birth to micro black holes. While debunked, somewhat, I knew I had to write a story about this. At the same time, I had just lost a close family member, and it didn't take long to marry those emotions with the potential craziness (or wonderfulness?) that a micro black hole could levy on the lives of people beset by grief.

When blocking out the story, I came across black-and-white photos of ancestors from nineteenth-century Russia, complete with heavy wool coats and ushankas, and boom, I had a setting. Since I'm not a scientist, the most difficult part for me was maintaining some fidelity to the universe's physical laws. That meant immersion in books by Brian Greene, Kip Thorne, and other physicists, and more than a few times asking stupid questions and creating bizarre hypotheticals on physics chat boards.

In the end, the story is not hard science fiction — and anyone who offered me advice on the chat boards would be mortified by what I've done — but the basic principles of gravity, time dilation, and relatively are fully at play and legit. In the end, this story is about a grandmother, her son, and her grandson, and the family staying connected through the interstitial spaces between known physical dimensions, despite the actions of a hostile government and the limitations of mortality.

A question for the author

Q: What's the story no one else thinks is as good as you do?

A: "City Dog, Country Frog", by Mo Willems, is a fan favorite for the five and under club, but it's a masterpiece for the more "sophisticated" audience as well. The structure is elegant, following a friendship between a dog and frog through four seasons, and the movement through the seasons parallels the arc of their friendship. The ending is as sad as an austere Cormac McCarthy ending, but has a twist that offers a glimmer of hope.

About the author

Esem Junior grew up in the long, dark winters of Upstate New York, one of the country's own Siberias. He is a former crime reporter, and writes speculative and other forms of literary fiction.

Copyright

Title information

Metaphorosis March 2021

ISSN: 2573-136X (online)
ISBN: 978-1-64076-195-7 (e-book)
ISBN: 978-1-64076-196-4 (paperback)

Copyright

Publisher

Metaphorosis
a magazine of speculative fiction

Metaphorosis Magazine is an imprint of
Metaphorosis Publishing
Neskowin, OR, USA

www.metaphorosis.com

"Metaphorosis" is a registered trademark.

Discounts available

Substantial discounts are available for educational institutions, including writing workshops. Discounts are also available for quantity purchases. For details, contact Metaphorosis at metaphorosis.com/about

Metaphorosis Publishing

Metaphorosis offers beautifully written science fiction and fantasy. Our imprints include:

Metaphorosis Magazine
Plant Based Press
Verdage

You can also find us:
@MetaphorosisMag, @MetaphorosisRev,
@Metaphorosis
www.facebook.com/metaphorosis

Help keep Metaphorosis running by supporting us at
Patreon.com/metaphorosis

See more about some of our books on the following pages.

Metaphorosis Magazine

Metaphorosis is an online speculative fiction magazine dedicated to quality writing. We publish an original story every week, along with author bios, interviews, and notes on story origins.

We also publish monthly print and e-book issues, as well as yearly Best of and Complete anthologies.

Come and see us online at magazine.Metaphorosis.com

Metaphorosis:
Best of 2020

The best science fiction and fantasy stories from *Metaphorosis* magazine's fifth year.

Metaphorosis
2020

All the stories from *Metaphorosis* magazine's fifth year. Fifty-two great SFF stories.

Metaphorosis:
Best of 2019

The best science fiction and fantasy stories from *Metaphorosis* magazine's fourth year.

Metaphorosis
2019

All the stories from *Metaphorosis* magazine's fourth year. Fifty-two great SFF stories.

Metaphorosis:
Best of 2018

The best science fiction and fantasy stories from *Metaphorosis* magazine's third year.

Metaphorosis
2018

All the stories from *Metaphorosis* magazine's third year. Fifty-two great SFF stories.

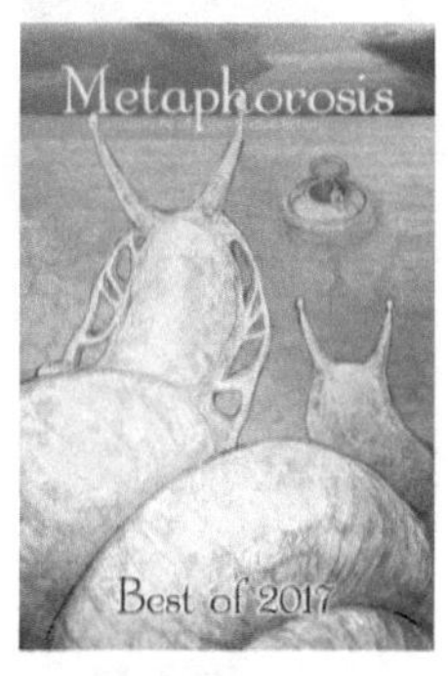 

Metaphorosis:
Best of 2017

The best science fiction and fantasy stories from *Metaphorosis* magazine's *second* year.

Metaphorosis
2017

All the stories from *Metaphorosis* magazine's second year. Fifty-three great SFF stories.

Metaphorosis:
Best of 2016

The best science fiction and fantasy stories from *Metaphorosis* magazine's first year.

Metaphorosis
2016

Almost all the stories from *Metaphorosis* magazine's first year.

Plant Based Press

Vegan-friendly science fiction and fantasy, including an annual anthology of the year's best SFF stories.

Best Vegan SFF of 2020

The best vegan-friendly science fiction and fantasy stories of 2020!

Best Vegan SFF of 2019

The best vegan-friendly science fiction and fantasy stories of 2019!

Best Vegan SFF of 2018

The best vegan-friendly science fiction and fantasy stories of 2018!

Best Vegan SFF of 2017

The best vegan-friendly science fiction and fantasy stories of 2017!

Best Vegan SFF of 2016

The best vegan-friendly science fiction and fantasy stories of 2016!

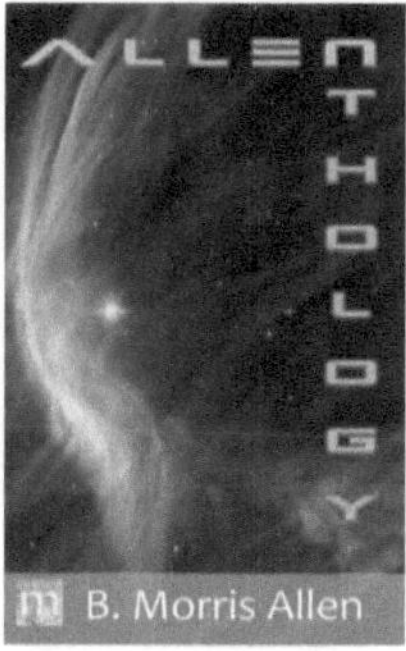

Susurrus

A darkly romantic story of magic, love, and suffering.

Allenthology: Volume I

A quarter century of SFF, including the full contents of the collections *Tocsin, Start with Stones,* and *Metaphorosis.*

Science fiction and fantasy books for writers – full of great stories, often with an additional focus on the craft of speculative fiction writing.

Reading 5X5 x2

Duets

How do authors' voices change when they collaborate?

A round-robin of five talented science fiction and fantasy authors collaborating with each other and writing solo.

Including stories by Evan Marcroft, David Gallay, J. Tynan Burke, L'Erin Ogle, and Douglas Anstruther.

Score

an SFF symphony

What if stories were written like music? *Score* is an anthology of varied stories arranged to follow an emotional score from the heights of joy to the depths of despair – but always with a little hope shining through.

Reading 5X5

Five stories, five times

Twenty-five SFF authors, five base stories, five versions of each – see how different writers take on the same material.

Reading 5X5

Writers' Edition

Two extra stories, the story seed, and authors' notes on writing. Over 100 pages of additional material specifically aimed at writers.

9 781640 761964